PRAISE FOR VIVIAN AREND

"If you've never read a Vivian Arend book you are missing out on one of the best contemporary authors writing today."
~ *Book Reading Gals*

A Firefighter's Christmas Gift is a sweet romance; a heart-warming and passionate Christmas story. The premise is inspiring and delightful: the romance is encouraging and sensual.
~The Reading Cafe

This is a wonderful love story, and it was a magical Christmas story. It was great to celebrate the holiday with the residents of heart falls.
~ Book Addict Live

"This story will keep you reading from the first page to the last one. There is never a dull moment..."
~ *Landy Jimenez*

"I definitely recommend to fans of contemporaries with hot cowboys and strong family ties.."
~ *SmexyBooks*

"This was my first Vivian Arend story, and I know I want more!"
~ *Red Hot Plus Blue Reads*

Another masterpiece of love and passion Ms. Arend and all I have to say is THANK YOU!
~Romance Witch Reviews

ALSO BY VIVIAN AREND

Holidays in Heart Falls

A Firefighter's Christmas Gift

A Soldier's Christmas Wish

A Hero's Christmas Hope

A Cowboy's Christmas List

A Rancher's Christmas Kiss

The Stones of Heart Falls

A Rancher's Heart

A Rancher's Song

A Rancher's Bride

A Rancher's Love

A Rancher's Vow

The Colemans of Heart Falls

The Cowgirl's Forever Love

The Cowgirl's Secret Love

The Cowgirl's Chosen Love

A full list of Vivian's print titles is available on her website

www.vivianarend.com

A RANCHER'S CHRISTMAS KISS

HOLIDAYS IN HEART FALLS: BOOK 5

VIVIAN AREND

This is a work of fiction. Names, characters, places, and incidents either are the product of the author's imagination or are used fictitiously, and any resemblance to any persons, living or dead, business establishments, events, or locales is entirely coincidental.

INTERLUDE

January 1, Heart Falls

The sidewalk leading to the church doors was covered with a thin layer of freshly fallen snow. Ashton Stewart snagged the shovel from against the brick wall and slowly worked to clear the path.

His breath escaped in a cloud of white, the crisp day beautiful beyond belief. January in Alberta could be meaner than a bear, but those lower temperatures typically rolled in later in the month. In line with the start of a new year, today was an ordinary cold. Which meant it was brisk enough to make each breath sear his lungs and his eyes to water.

Pretty as a postcard, though, with the recent snowfall clinging to the spruce trees. If he could have ordered a blue-sky day like this one, he would have.

Ashton snorted at his musings. As if *he* were in charge. If he could order the world to turn the way he wanted it to, he'd have gotten to this point in his life a hell of a lot sooner than sixty-five.

Of course, that would have required being a hell of a lot *smarter* sooner as well. It appeared he was the type who needed the lessons hammered in hard for them to finally register.

His phone vibrated in his pocket. He scrambled to grab it, the shovel falling unminded to the ground.

Not a call. Not an email. Damn technology. What the hell did *vibrate* mean again?

Right. Ashton checked his messages and found one from his nephew.

Tucker: *Where are you?*

Ashton didn't want to respond, but he should. They did work together, and there might be an emergency…

He shook his head. What he was doing right now was *the* most important thing. Tucker would have to deal with any trouble that arose right now.

Determined, Ashton texted back.

Ashton: *I've got the rest of the day off.*

Tucker: *Great. Fine. Now answer my question.*

Ashton: *I'm busy.*

Tucker: *Good grief, at least tell me you're at the church.*

Ashton: *Yes, I'm here. That's spooky.*

Tucker: *That's the pastor accidentally texting me instead of you. He's running late. Says you should use the spare key to unlock the place and let yourself in. The key is behind the rose bush by the kitchen door.*

Ashton: *Thanks.*

Tucker: *At the risk of overstepping, everything okay? You need some company?*

Ashton paused then answered: *Everything will be fine. And you probably shouldn't come because if what I hope for happens, it should be an all-or-nothing deal. I'll explain later.*

Tucker: *Okay. Fingers crossed if it helps.*

Ashton turned off his phone to avoid any further interruptions then tucked it away.

If Sonora took him up on the invitation to meet him, everything *would* be fine. He had to believe it, no matter how impossible that seemed after all these years.

It only took a moment to unlock the side door and slip inside.

Ashton had never been in the church alone before. It was a humbling experience walking in silence through the chapel. A place to reflect, consider, and hopefully do something to turn the tide on the nightmarish dreams he'd recently experienced.

His fingers shook as he unlocked the main doors.

Quarter to twelve.

He stepped outside to ensure the doors were both unlocked and opened easily. It only took a moment to remove and hang up his outer coat before he returned to the sanctuary, wandering as slowly as possible toward the altar.

Sunlight streamed in the stained-glass windows, leaving brightly coloured patches all the way down the aisle. Quiet hung on the air, the still, solemn hush broken only by the faint sound of wind against the tall steeple.

Dressed in his best suit, with polished boots and his hair combed back as neat as it ever got, Ashton would've felt like a fool except for the pounding in his heart.

He glanced at his watch. Five minutes to noon.

Maybe he should pray. This was the place for it, wasn't it? Maybe prayer was what he needed to make his miracle come true.

He examined every inch of the room as he pivoted on the spot. Some candles and decorations remained from the holiday season. In the corner of the front platform, bright tinsel glittered on the tree, the star at the top slightly off-kilter. Such an ordinary place for the extraordinary to happen.

Please, God.

That was the sum of his prayers. He couldn't improve on it one bit.

Another peek at his watch.

Two more minutes to wait.

Two minutes until he'd know if he'd found the truth in time to save his soul.

Two minutes until Sonora arrived.

Or didn't—

The door clicked open behind him, and he whirled toward the sunshine.

THE GHOSTS OF CHRISTMAS PAST

December, eighteen years ago

*H*appy chaos danced through the halls and upstairs rooms of the Fields' new home in Heart Falls. The family matriarch, Sonora Fallen, smiled in anticipation as she stood at the front door and took in the laughter, excited shouts, and happy background music.

Mid-December was late for first-day-of-school jitters, but they would deal with it.

Then she went looking for her oldest granddaughter, who she knew would be as far from the noise and bustle as possible.

Sure enough, fourteen-year-old Ivy was curled up in an oversized chair tucked into the corner of the new family room. Delicate as always, at this moment her pale cheeks were flushed bright red. She had her backpack on the table in front of her and a brush in her hand.

Sonora settled on the footstool. "Want me to braid your hair?"

"Yes, please, Grandma."

They switched positions. Sonora examined the thin shoulders before her, noticing with pride how the girl held herself upright, her breathing calm and even.

Sonora pulled the brush through Ivy's long white-blonde hair slowly, appreciating how even though the house was full of life and love, this little corner was quiet and peaceful. Just what Ivy needed.

Which meant it was part of what Sonora needed—why she'd accompanied her daughter and son-in-law and family on their move to this small town. Fingers crossed that soon Sonora's chicks would be settled and happy in their new home here in Heart Falls.

"Ready for school?" she asked as she started on Ivy's braid.

"I am. I guess," Ivy added softly. "I know moving when we did was best for Tansy, and I'm really glad we took the couple of months to get to know her while we homeschooled. But I'm a little afraid that because we moved so late, it's going to be hard to make new friends. Everyone else has been together since September."

Sonora snorted indelicately. "Not that you want this reminder, darling, but this is a very small town. Everyone else might have been together since *kindergarten*. I doubt starting in September would have changed much."

Ivy gasped then laughed. "That doesn't make my first-day stress levels better. You're terrible, Grandma."

"I'm honest," Sonora returned. "Which is why, when I tell you the second part, you can absolutely trust that I'm not pulling a fast one. I hear you and your concerns. I have some of those same worries, you know. I'm beginning again as well, and I don't have school to line people up for me to find kindred spirits."

Ivy tilted her head. "I forgot you need to find new friends too."

"We're both entitled to be a little anxious." Sonora tightened the elastic then paused to take Ivy's face in her hands. "The second part I want you to remember is that not everyone needs to like you. One friend. *One* friendly face is all we need to start the journey."

"For you too?"

Sonora nodded. "I'll tell you as soon as I find that one friend. And you do the same, okay? We can cheer each other on."

Ivy dipped her chin. "Okay."

Sonora smoothed the braid back, the long length falling nearly to Ivy's waist. The instant she was done, her granddaughter hugged Sonora fiercely. "I love you, Grandma."

"Love you too. Now let's go find Rose and Tansy and see if your sisters are prepared for their junior high debut."

"At least they have each other," Ivy said wistfully before ducking away from Sonora's tickling fingers. "I know, I know. One friendly face."

Half an hour later, Malachi's voice boomed as he summoned the family. "Front door, everyone. I need a picture for the family album."

There were the usual wiggles and squirming to get them in place. Sonora smiled in amusement as she beheld her three oldest granddaughters.

Ivy stood to one side calmly, only the white-knuckle grip on her sky-blue coat giving away her nerves. In contrast, the two twelve-year-olds beside her buzzed with energy. Rose's long dark hair held barely any wave, she'd tamed it so hard. Next to her, Tansy's dirty-blonde hair stuck up in an unruly bob, and her eyes flashed before she offered a tilted grin and looped an arm around Rose's shoulders.

Ivy's skin was whiter than white, Tansy's shades of pale cream, and Rose's a light brown. Their shirts were green, yellow, and red.

Their mother, Sophie, laughed out loud then shifted the three-year-old in her arms to the other hip. "You girls dressed to match your names. You should have told me. I would have put Fern in green as well."

Malachi gestured frantically. "Timer is on. Family portrait in ten, nine, eight..."

All seven of them crowded together. Fern leaned sideways in her mom's arms, catching hold of Sonora and impulsively kissing her grandma's cheek just as the flash went off.

"To the car," Sophie announced, passing Fern to Malachi. "Grandma is driving. She and I have some exploring to do after you're all checked in."

Tansy and Rose paused to kiss their youngest sister goodbye. Ivy stayed by the door and gave Fern a heartfelt finger wiggle that the toddler answered with generous air kisses.

By the time the girls were dropped off at school, Sonora was ready to suggest a coffee with a kicker to calm her own nerves.

Her daughter seemed to agree. Sophie peered out the window and examined the shops going past. "Is there time for coffee? I could use a jolt of caffeine."

"What about the diner on Second Street?" Sonora frowned as she headed in that direction. "I don't know that I saw any other options."

"Heart Falls is a lot smaller than Calgary, but I think the pros will outweigh the cons in the long run."

S & J Café was the same layout and decor as every small-town mom-and-pop operation Sonora had ever seen. Same beige-white ceramic mugs she'd seen in a million church cupboards. Same metal chairs with plastic seat cushions, same fake-wood tables in the booths. There was a comfort in that sameness, though. Sonora didn't disapprove.

When the tired-looking waitress filled their cups with a black liquid Sonora assumed was coffee, she held in her amusement.

Sophie eyed her cup before sipping cautiously. The speed with which she reached for the sugar bowl and ripped open three more packages said it all.

"That good?"

"It's very...exciting." Sophie blinked hard then spoke softly. "We'll set up a coffee station at the bookstore for Malachi. He'll never survive otherwise."

"Smart move. Nothing big enough to rock the boat, but a chance to give people with taste buds an option." Sonora sipped from her own cup then gasped. "Oh, no. Forget about not rocking the boat." She leaned in close. "Can I convince you to open a coffee shop instead of a bookstore?"

Sophie laughed. "Nope. Now tell me more about your plans. I know the sale is confirmed. When do you officially own the house in the country?"

Sonora leaned back against the plastic-covered bench, abandoned the coffee, and focused on the delightful new adventure about to arrive. "January first. It's a little unreal, though. Just think, I own a parcel of land, a barn and arena, and a four-bedroom house. I'm so thrilled I can't even describe the sensation."

"I can't believe you're really doing it," Sophie said then quickly raised her hand. "Scratch that. I can definitely believe it, and I'm happy for you, Mom. I've adored having your help with the girls, especially during these past six months while we dealt with Tansy's adoption and welcomed her into the family. But you deserve to have your own place and not be at my beck and call all the time."

"Being a help has been a joy," Sonora said. "But it's time for you to enjoy your family without me constantly underfoot. That's important too, you know. Making your own traditions. Plus, you and Malachi finally get to talk things out without another opinion intruding."

"You're not an intrusion," her adopted daughter insisted,

"and Malachi would say the same thing. But I will agree to you not living with us as long as you promise to visit as much as you'd like. If you're ever lonely, come over. Please?"

Sonora squeezed her hand. "Of course. I love all of you, and I plan to get at least a weekly dose of family."

Their meals arrived. The food was good and hearty, and as they ate, they talked in the easy way of family who liked each other. At only nine years apart, Sonora had always felt her role as more a guide than a parental figure to Sophie.

Deep-toned laughter billowed from the corner of the restaurant, and they both turned to examine the group of men gathered there.

Six or seven of them, a couple standing as they chatted with the ones seated at the table. Men of the land, Sonora guessed from the sturdy winter coats and cowboy hats on the ones who'd stopped to talk.

A couple of them sported beards that needed trimming. Sonora kept her opinion to herself, or at least she planned on it until Sophie leaned over and whispered, "Santas in training for those two, you think?"

"Terrible child." Although Sonora knew where the younger woman had gotten it from. She winked at her daughter. "You might be right. They can use the next twenty years to master the look."

"They probably have it, although if they don't do some grooming before then, they'll end up Rip van Winkle instead of Kris Kringle."

One of the men standing shifted position, and Sonora's attention sharpened on the final person in the gathering.

Now there was an attractive man. Clean-shaven, about her age, she guessed, with dark hair and tanned skin. He definitely wore the outdoors on his skin, but it suited him. A little rough around the edges, but she'd always liked that in a man. Good to know there were some finer gentlemen in town to admire.

Not that she had any interest in dating. She was going to own and live in a house by herself for the first time ever. There was enough excitement in that to satisfy anyone.

She focused her attention back on her daughter and enjoyed the moment.

The morning passed in a blur. Sophie returned to the house, while Sonora did a few more chores before heading to pick up the girls. Tansy and Rose would eventually walk the short distance home, but Ivy—it would depend on how her health was.

But on the first day? Everyone got a ride.

A few minutes early, Sonora wandered in the main doors of the school, planning to examine the holiday information and the art displays near the main office.

Unexpectedly, Ivy sat to the side of the hall. She already wore her coat and boots, and her hands rested in her lap, gaze unfocused on the wall opposite the bench.

Sonora settled beside her and linked their fingers together. "Tough day?"

Her granddaughter blinked as if surprised to discover her there. "Hi, Grandma. No, it wasn't bad."

Okay... "You're ready to go early, though."

"The teacher suggested I take my things and get out of the rush before the halls got crowded." Ivy wrinkled her nose and spoke softly. "I think she was trying to be helpful because some kids were mean."

The question was how mean, and could Sonora convince her daughter, and herself, that casting the Wrath of Mom on the culprits might not be the best solution?

"They had a test today, which I didn't have to take," Ivy continued. "And then it was cold enough that I stayed in at lunch. At my big desk at the back of the room that I didn't have to share."

"Uh-oh," Sonora offered.

Ivy sighed. "Someone decided I should be called *Icy* instead of *Ivy*."

Her granddaughter lifted her free hand to wipe at her eyes, and Sonora reconsidered any thoughts of giving the kids a break. Teenagers could be such nasty creatures.

But then something amazing happened. Ivy squeezed her fingers. "But I made a friend."

Sonora blinked. "You did?"

Ivy nodded. "Before lunch was over, this boy came back into the room. His name is Walker, and he asked if it was okay if we talked."

Curious. Not only the story, but the fact a hint of colour had returned to Ivy's cheeks. "And was it okay?" Sonora asked.

Her granddaughter gave a quick nod. "He lives on a ranch just outside Heart Falls. He has three brothers and a sister, and they raise horses and cattle, and they have barns—" Ivy peeked at Sonora, flushing even brighter. "He said his sister, Ginny, would be in Rose and Tansy's class, along with her best friend, Dare, and that we should all come to the ranch for a visit sometime. His parents like to have people over."

"Well, that was very considerate." Sonora patted Ivy's hand then stood before guiding her toward the door. "We'll have to give them a call sometime."

"I have their number." Ivy dug in her pocket and pulled out a folded piece of notepaper. "Walker said I should get Mom to call his mom tonight because it's going to get busy with the holidays, and he really wanted—" The girl's cheeks grew even redder, but she swallowed hard, and even though she stared at the floor as she spoke, she got the words out. "He really wanted me to see the ranch."

Something more important was happening than Ivy being impressed by the kind young man. That the girl with social anxiety was willing to get together with virtual strangers?

It appeared forward steps would be taken rapidly in this new town of theirs.

Sonora nodded with approval. "Well, then. I guess we'll give them a call."

1

———

*I*t made sense, Ashton Stewart supposed, considering Silver Stone ranch had been in operation for a touch over twenty years, and he'd been a part of it from the start.

All he knew for sure was this was his favourite stall. The one where, with only a few steps or a strategic pivot of his head, he had a clear view of everyone coming or going through the main barn.

As foreman, he needed to stay on top of matters. But more than that, he *liked* knowing. Liked to be helpful and ahead of the game when it came to not only his job but in being there for the people he cared about.

Which meant he knew the exact moment Walter Stone stepped out of the tack room. Tall and sturdy, with skin that was tanned from hours of outdoor labour, Silver Stone's co-owner brushed his hands on his thighs as he slowly paced the corridor, gaze drifting over the horses, a contented smile on his face.

A good man, Ashton's boss. Someone Ashton willingly called a friend as well.

Walter paused beside the open stall door, petting Lonesome

Charlie on the nose as he spoke to the animal Ashton was currying. "You're a spoiled old man, aren't you?"

"Well, that's a fine way to talk to your foreman," Ashton mock grumbled. "Who're you calling old?"

Walter laughed, soothing the surprised horse with a few clicks of his tongue. "Definitely not you, considering that would be painting me with the same brush. We're eternally young, you and I."

"Much better." Ashton kept working but glanced pointedly. "You look done for the day."

"I guess I am. Deb told me to make sure I stopped on time. I don't have the guts to show up less than half an hour early when she lays down the law."

"Smart man," Ashton returned.

Although it wasn't because the man's wife was a hellion. No, Deb was wonderful, and keeping on her good side was out of respect rather than fear. Unlike some…

"When you're done, come to the house and join us," Walter offered. "We're having a barbecue for some new neighbours."

Ashton continued currying the horse, amusement growing. "Hate to tell you this, boss, but you've mixed up your seasons."

"Caleb said the same thing, so his sister told him she'd make the chili extra spicy to make up for the snow on the ground." Walter leaned on the stall doorpost, folding his arms over his chest. "The new family has kids nearly the same age as my three youngest if you can believe it. But Deb said after talking with their mom that an outdoor event with some room to spread out would work best. So we're lighting a bonfire, pulling out the sleds, and preparing for a bit of a free-for-all."

"Sounds like an adventure. I'd love to come say hello, although I might not stay long." Ashton grinned at his boss. "Ginny's spicy chili is a selling feature. Even at twelve, that girl's got some chops in the kitchen. Simple fare, but killer."

"Then we'll see you later." Walter dipped his chin and slowly paced away, whistling as he went.

There was always something going on at the Stone household. With five kids—the oldest at twenty-one and the youngest, five—it was to be expected. Ashton pulled the brush over Lonesome Charlie's withers slowly, contentedly finishing his task.

Silver Stone ranch had been a good home for him as well, and Ashton counted his blessings every day. Getting to watch the family grow over the years had been a treat, especially considering he'd never had one of his own.

Not that he'd missed having one. Not really. It had never been one of his goals.

His thoughts drifted as he completed his final tasks and made sure the ranch hands on night duty were all in place and settled. Ashton stepped into the warmth of his private rooms at the end of the long bunkhouse row. He washed up quickly so he could head over to the main ranch house.

He was pulling on his boots when the phone rang. He grabbed it quickly, the cord tangling as he propped the receiver against his shoulder and went back to his boots. "Ashton."

"Hello. Did I catch you at a good moment?" His older brother spoke quickly. "I won't keep you long."

"Hey, Steve. I've got a couple minutes. How's everything? How's my favourite nephew doing?"

"Tucker is your only nephew," Steve said dryly. "We're all physically well. Tucker's grade point average is dismal, though, so Lynn and I registered him in a scholastic bootcamp over the holidays. Hopefully that will improve his grades before the school year is complete."

Poor kid. The sixteen-year-old was a natural with animals, yet Ashton's brother and his wife seemed determined to turn him into an academic like themselves.

"Make sure he gets some outdoor fun as well, right?

Teenage boys think better if they get to burn off physical energy first."

A long-suffering sigh echoed over the phone. "Considering we have a child and you don't, excuse me if I don't take your parenting advice."

"Bullshit on me not having kids. I'm basically dad to a dozen hands here at the ranch," Ashton countered. "Just give Tucker a break. That's all I'm saying."

"Anyway," Steve went on. "Lynn and I are scheduling for next year and need to confirm. You'll take Tucker for the summer again?"

"Of course." Ashton enjoyed having the kid around more than he'd ever expected. Plus, he knew his nephew lived for getting to spend time with his Stone friends. Now to say yes in the way his brother needed to hear. "Truthfully, Silver Stone plans to expand production next year. All the boys will be old enough to help, so thanks for letting me have him. I'll be sure he learns lots."

"That's fine. I need to go. Take care."

The phone clicked off, dial tone buzzing in Ashton's ear.

He hung up, shaking his head as he pulled on his warmest coat to head to the gathering.

It was a pity the strongest connection he had with Steve was his nephew. Ashton was grateful for Tucker, even as he wondered how on earth he and his brother could be so very different in so many ways. They didn't dislike each other, but there wasn't a lot that Ashton admired about the man either.

Still pondering, Ashton crossed the snowy yard to where a crowd of kids were crawling up and down the short hill beyond the ranch house. The oldest, Caleb, pulled a sled that held his youngest brother, Dusty, and a small figure dressed in bright pink. The ride involved much arm waving on the five-year-old's part, and sweet little-girl laughter rose from the newcomer sitting with Dusty.

Ashton nodded a greeting to Walter as he made his way to be introduced to the new family.

The tall Black man beside Walter laughed in response to some comment, curling his arm around the thin white woman with blond hair at his side.

Another woman with creamy-white skin stood nearby as well, a gentle smile on her lips as she stared over the yard to where the children were playing. This second one had long light-blond hair, with a thick strand of silver-grey in the front. She didn't have the same facial features as the younger woman, but maybe she was an older sister?

"Ah, there he is." Walter gestured to Ashton, and all three newcomers turned toward him. "Silver Stone's foreman and our good friend, Ashton Stewart. Ashton, come meet some new neighbours."

The tall man extended his hand. "Malachi Fields. This is my wife, Sophie."

"Good to meet you both. Welcome." Ashton shook the man's hand and then Sophie's.

A loud shriek sounded from the tobogganing slope. They turned in time to see the second oldest of Walter's boys bounce to his feet and wave in their direction. "It's okay. Everybody's okay," Luke shouted, pulling a laughing pile of girls apart from where two sleds had collided at the base of the hill.

"The little ones weren't in that crash, I take it?" Sophie asked.

"Caleb has them," Ashton assured her, pointing to the side of the hill. "He's a solid young man. He'll take good care of them. Is your youngest with him?"

"Fern. She's three," Malachi shared. He glanced around then pointed at the two girls scrambling up the hill with Luke and his sister. "Tansy and Rose, both twelve."

"And Ivy is our oldest at fourteen," Sophie said. "Walker took her to see the horses."

Ashton nodded then turned his attention on the final person he needed to greet.

Sophie continued. "And this is my mother, Sonora Fallen."

Mother.

The hell?

Ashton glanced between the two women. How was that possible? Sophie looked maybe in her early- to mid-thirties. No way was Sonora older than Ashton, let alone in her fifties. Her blue eyes were bright with a silvery sheen that danced with mischief. Laugh lines creased the corners, but nothing like she should have to be the grandmother to a fourteen-year-old.

Sonora raised a brow. "There a problem?"

Jeez. Ashton had been staring. What's worse, the woman had put her hand out, and he'd already taken it and yet was standing there motionless, her fingers trapped in his.

"Sorry," he said quickly, shaking her hand. "Welcome to Heart Falls. It's a great little town. Still some growing to do, but you should find everything you need to be comfortable. I hope you'll settle in well."

"We'll try our best. But I'm not living in town."

"Sonora bought the old rental property on the next range road over," Walter informed him. "You were wondering who was moving in."

Ashton prided himself on being quick on his feet but somehow found himself at a loss for words. "The old Crofter place?"

"That's the one," Sonora said happily, turning to Walter. "I plan to do something with my land, but it's probably more than I need. You said you might have an idea?"

"We used to hay the outer ranges. If you want, I'll have Ashton get in touch with you to explain when we'll cultivate, and cut, and the rest of it. That's the deal we've had in place with other neighbours over the years."

"Sounds wonderful." Sonora's focus landed on Ashton.

"When should we meet? I'm free most days this week, so whenever works for you."

He mumbled a bit, tongue and brain refusing to coordinate.

Walter's cocky grin didn't help matters, and Ashton glared briefly before managing to offer a suggestion that Sonora accepted immediately.

Malachi and the ladies paced away to meet with another family coming across the yard to join them, leaving Walter and Ashton alone.

A soft snicker drifted from his friend.

Ashton casually swung his elbow and tagged Walter in the ribs, hard.

Snickering slid to a gasping laugh. "I'm sorry," Walter offered. "But your face was priceless there for a moment. I've never seen you so gobsmacked before in my life." Walter slapped a hand on Ashton's shoulder to guide him toward the barbecue tucked against the side of the house.

"Not gobsmacked. Confused, though," Ashton admitted. "That's Sophie's *mother*?"

"I've got no idea how either," Walter said easily. "Guess you can find out more when you're chatting up the fine Ms. Fallen this week during your date."

Ashton whipped his head toward the other man and glared. "It's not a date."

Walter didn't say anything. Just turned on the barbecue and began whistling as he prepared to scrub the racks clean.

"You're an ass," Ashton grumbled.

Walter laughed again, the way Ashton knew he would. "Probably." He made eye contact and grinned wider. "But an ass who sees an opportunity developing that only a fool would ignore."

Yet *ignoring* was the smartest option at this point. No matter how fine the new neighbour was. Ashton needed more time to think and consider before he made any assumptions or decisions.

He wasn't looking for his life to change. Not really.

"Get the food and I'll finish this." Ashton stole the barbecue brush from Walter then pushed him aside. A nice mindless task that let both his gaze and mind wander. And if both moved to consider Sonora...

So be it.

2

____

The farm wasn't officially hers for another few weeks, but when Sonora stopped by the office to arrange another visit, the realtor simply gave her a key.

"The house is empty. I see no reason you shouldn't go ahead and take measurements. May as well get yourself ready to move as soon as the bank gives the final go-ahead." The woman offered a friendly wave then let Sonora head out alone to her soon-to-be home.

Small towns. Got to love them.

Sonora stopped in front of the door, suddenly wondering if it was even locked. Sure enough, the knob turned easily under her fingers, and she shook her head with more amusement than concern.

Small towns, indeed.

The door hinges complained shrilly when she stepped into the front hall. She paused to hang her coat on one of the readily available hooks.

A slow wander through the house followed, Sonora nearly giddy with excitement as she paced. It was more than she needed, but the price had been right. Two simple bedrooms were tucked in the back. With windows that faced the eastern side of the property, the rooms would fill with sunshine each morning. The shared bathroom between them held a counter with double sinks and a smaller tub-shower combination.

To the north was the primary bedroom with an attached bath that had everything Sonora could want except a soaker tub. And a final fourth bedroom with what she'd call an oversized nursery took up the final leg of the sleeping quarters.

At the front of the house, the neat kitchen didn't need any improvements other than adding some knickknacks to give it some character. The cozy space next to it would work wonderfully with either a built-in nook or a long trestle table.

The star feature of the house, though, was the living room. A wood-burning stove, plenty of room for couches, and a breathtaking view. The windows faced the western mountains, with kilometers of open prairie in front and to the sides of her home with no visible signs of civilization.

The lone piece of furniture in the house was a rickety old chair, and Sonora dropped into it, mesmerized by the landscape.

"Greg, you would have loved this," she told the ghost of her husband.

Leaning back, legs stretched in front of her, she considered all the moments that had led to this one. Travelling, falling in love, building a family with Greg, and then losing him suddenly. The years when she'd raised her adopted daughter alone and then eventually helped with Sophie's growing family.

Silence buzzed in Sonora's ears. She went motionless, listening as hard as she could.

Nothing.

No voices, no laughter.

Not only were the sounds of humans absent, so were the lighter background noises that existed in homes with multiple people. Here and now, the floorboards lay silent. No washing machine or dishwasher or taps running or music playing. The buzz of appliances was absent, and with no wind outside, any branches that might tap on walls or windows remained still.

Utter quiet.

A smile arrived, tugging the corners of her lips upward, and a heady dose of contentment rolled over her from head to toe.

"This is what I need. For now, at least," she said, speaking out loud as she occasionally did to Greg. He had been gone for longer than he'd been her husband, but the habit remained. "The years of being with Sophie and watching her family grow have been a privilege, and I'm not giving that up. But this?"

She took a deep inhale then released it so slowly that her heartbeat was the only noise in the universe.

Bang, bang, bang.

Sonora jerked upright in shock at the loud, impetuous racket at her front door. The chair under her rebelled at the sudden move, and one of the legs gave way.

"*Oh.*" She tumbled, air propelling from her lungs as the chair seat hit the ground, her ass right on top of it.

The front door jerked open, the rusty hinges offering a scream like a wild animal caught in a trap. A deep voice sounded. "Sonora?"

She pulled herself to a seated position and blinked hard at Ashton Stewart as he rushed across the open floorboards to her side.

"Hi." Casual, calm. At least that's the attitude she tried for.

He stalled in the middle of reaching for her. The concern in his eyes turned to confusion. "Hi. You okay?"

She held a hand to him. "Sure. Just checking the floorboards for structural integrity."

His strong fingers wrapped around hers, and he gently tugged her to her feet. "The floor looks fine. The chair on the other hand..."

"You know the story of Goldilocks? I've often wondered what went through her mind during her mission of mischief." Sonora brushed dirt and splinters from her slacks. "Now I can honestly say she wouldn't have been left unscathed by the breaking-chair part of the adventure. Which is good."

"Most people consider being chased by bears sufficient punishment," Ashton said dryly.

"I'm not most people." Feeling more like herself, she lifted her gaze to his without embarrassment. "I'd offer you a seat, but since I've removed that possibility, welcome to my future home."

The man rotated in a slow circle. "You've done amazing things with it."

Laughter bubbled free. His dry tone of voice, his comment —all of it hit her funny bone just right. The edge of reserve she'd pulled on because of his odd behavior during their first meeting melted slightly.

Sonora stepped toward the window. "Inside, I will eventually have what I need. But I hope you can help with my outdoor needs."

"Which would be?" He paused. "Walter already mentioned we can hay your excess land, but I'm asking what you're thinking of in terms of animals. Do you plan to run livestock? Want to breed racehorses?"

Another rush of excitement struck. "I really can do anything I want, can't I?"

Concern replaced his previously neutral expression. "Well, it's true on one level. You've got some room to work with." He paused. "Any experience?"

Poor man. Sonora decided to put him out of his misery. "Sorry, I wasn't truly talking about going into business. I'm just excited about the opportunities out there." She considered for a moment. "I'd like to learn how to ride. And how to take care of a horse and all that involves. And maybe get a dog," she added before he could respond.

"You don't ride?"

She shook her head. "I have in the past. A few times, but I wouldn't call myself a horsewoman. I'm not afraid of them, though."

"Doesn't mean you should own one." He dragged a hand through his hair. "Okay, leave the horse idea for a minute. A dog—what kind of dog? Inside or out?"

It was too tempting. "Oh, definitely one that I can have both places. One with curly fur, about so big?" She held a hand above the floor, indicating a medium-large creature. "I think they're called doodles. They look very intelligent and kind. I bet they'd love living on a farm."

His lips tightened. He'd removed his hat and now clutched the brim, holding on so tight his knuckles had gone white. "A *doodle*. On a farm."

"My farm," Sonora said brightly. "To be friends with my horse. And definitely some cats, and maybe a few chickens, and—"

"Sonora," he interrupted. "Have you ever taken care of animals before?"

"Some," she said, flashing back to her time in the Peace Corps. She'd met her husband and daughter in Uganda, and for the first three years of their marriage, they'd raised nearly everything they'd eaten.

Ashton inhaled, deep and slow.

Poor man. She was about to offer up an "I'm teasing" comment, at least about the dog, when he took a very wrong turn.

He straight-up stood in her house, looked her in the eye, and told her what to do.

"You're not thinking about this clearly, so let me help you out. I have a lot of experience in this area." His tone of voice was calm yet condescending, as if he were speaking to a confused child. "You want one of those frou-frou dogs, fine, but it stays in the house. That's unless you want it to be fodder for the coyotes and wolves in the area. Come the spring, you can try your hand at chickens, but it's a lot more work than most people think. And you're definitely not buying a horse right off the bat. You can borrow a horse from Silver Stone for a while. Make sure you truly want the trouble. Plus, someone can help you with the saddling and heavy lifting." He pushed his hat back on his head and lifted his chin in a challenge. "Plant a garden. That's enough excitement to start."

All her earlier reservations about the man flooded back in. "Wow. That's quite the healthy collection of opinions you've voiced. Want to tell me anything else? Like what vehicle to buy or who to make friends with here in Heart Falls? I know"—she lifted a finger in the air—"you can help me plan where to plant my field of fucks. But then again, I'm pretty sure it's not going to grow anything in the next while."

He frowned as he considered. "Field of fuc—" His face reddened even as he stalled and frowned harder.

"As in *I don't have any fucks to give*?" Sonora offered airily before clicking her tongue and shaking her head. But when she spoke again, it was without malice. "I was kidding about the in- and out-of-house dog. Don't you have a sense of humour?"

"Apparently not," Ashton returned easily, but his lips turned upward. "Sorry. I'm used to handing out orders to my men, and while I have good ideas, I should remember you're a grown woman."

"Apology accepted. You do have some good ideas," Sonora said. "Borrowing a horse from Silver Stone would be fine at the start. I don't need to do everything at once."

"I'll give you my number. Once you've got things set up here at the farm and you have some free time, give me a call. I'll make sure someone's around to help and show you the ropes."

Much better. Sonora pulled a piece of paper and a pen from her purse and took down his information before asking if he could check out the barn next door to the house.

"I do have some experience raising animals," she assured him as they entered the cool quiet of the barn. "But I'm not looking to be self-sufficient. I've done that before, and it is rewarding. But I'll have enough on my plate as it is between spending time with the family and helping at the bookstore. Oh, and hopefully making some new friends."

Ashton opened one of the pens, eyeing the hinges as he swung the gate back and forth a few times. "At the risk of overstepping, again, there are some good people in town, but the best way to meet *your* people would be to get involved with activities you like. Otherwise, you might meet some great people you have nothing in common with."

"It'd be hard to find reasons to get together in that case, wouldn't it?"

He chuckled. "My brother still cannot figure out why his invitations to join him and his wife for bridge never make me eager to drop everything and rush over."

"Does he live close?" Sonora asked.

"Nearly a day's drive away, thank God."

It was her turn to laugh. "No contract bridge for you."

"Again, thank God." Ashton looked thoughtful. "To be clear, he's not a terrible person. We don't get along all the time, though."

"I feel as if by the time you reach our age, you don't have to get along with everyone all the time."

"If you do, one of you is probably not needed." Ashton eyed her. "You know, my boss was making noises about how you and I would make a great couple."

"Really? And what kind of noises were *you* making? Would you like to get involved with me?"

Ashton grinned. "That's blunt."

"Another thing about being an adult. If I'm curious, I ask. Saves time."

"I'm all for being efficient." He looked her over for a moment. Nothing rude in the gesture, especially considering the appreciation in his eyes. "Am I looking to get involved with you? At this point, no. I have a lot of responsibilities at Silver Stone, plus I like my life the way it is. I'm not interested in a long-term romantic relationship."

Zero insult in his words.

He flashed a smile in her direction, and for one moment, she paused and stared back. The attractive rough edges were there, and if she'd been looking for some fun, he'd have been a fine temptation to indulge in.

But glancing around the barn was more than enough of a thrill for her right now. She took a deep breath as she held on to the railing and peered up into the hayloft. "Well, that's convenient. Because what I would like is a friend. It's been nearly twenty years since I lived on a farm, and that wasn't in Canada. I have a lot to learn, but I look forward to the challenge."

When she turned to meet his gaze again, his expression had sharpened. "Speaking of being curious, how come you have a daughter nearly the same age as you?"

"I volunteered in the Peace Corps when I was eighteen. A widower with a nine-year-old daughter came to run the project, and we fell in love. Greg died suddenly ten years after we got married—a heart attack—and then it was just me and Sophie. Eventually she and Malachi fell in love, and when they started adopting, I was there to help."

Ashton nodded slowly. "Someday you'll have to tell me more about your time out of the country."

"I'd like that."

Then damn if he didn't reach his hand toward her. "Well,

then, welcome to Heart Falls. I'll do what I can to make settling in easier for you."

Which was why that night Sonora was able to assure her oldest granddaughter that she too had made a friend.

"And not a friend I expected either. Which makes me think Heart Falls is a wonderful place for us to set down roots."

Ivy looked up at her with overly bright eyes. "It's still hard to be somewhere new."

"It is. But many good things are hard. They're worth every bit of energy we put into them. Finding a new home, making new friends." Sonora squeezed her granddaughter's fingers. "Spending time with family so they know you love them."

Ivy gave a small laugh. "Oh, Grandma."

Sonora kissed her granddaughter then returned to her plots and plans. Daydreaming how to arrange the furniture in her new home. Dreaming about what animals to get down the road. Planning the garden she would plant. Which made her think of Ashton again.

Too many things made her think of Ashton.

I'm glad you have a friend, but don't you wish for something more?

She wasn't sure if the thought was hers or from the ghost of her husband. The only thing she was sure of was—*No.* She really *didn't* want anything more than friendship.

Not right now anyway.

The truth of that gave her a solid, happy place to stand.

3

People always said that time flew faster the older one got. If that continued to be true, Ashton dreaded his twilight years, because as it was, days passed so quickly, life was a blur.

The holidays were over; then suddenly it was spring. Snow clung to the shadowy edges of the fields. Grazing land turned into sloppy messes, while tiny purple crocuses poked their heads above the prairie grass.

Newborns were everywhere. Kittens in the hayloft, calves in the field. Beautiful colts and fillies in the barn—new bloodlines that, with some luck, might someday change Silver Stone's fortunes.

Canada Day arrived, and with it a combination of adrenaline and annoyance on Ashton's part. There was always a lot to be done around Silver Stone, and the animals didn't care what day it was on the calendar.

Same as they didn't give a damn what a man had done the night before—hangovers were not forgiven. Especially when feed and water didn't show up on time. Ashton started his morning doing other people's chores followed by lecturing and reprimanding the hands who had tied one on far too hard the previous evening.

When lunch rolled around, he was ready for a break. It was time to put aside being Silver Stone's foreman for a bit and just be Ashton.

He left a couple of well-chastised hands polishing saddles as he whistled his way out of the barn to the Canada Day gathering.

Ginny Stone had just turned thirteen, but the girl had a green thumb and a love for social events. Between the two traits, she'd wrangled some fine mischief. She been planting a huge garden with her mom for the past few years. And this holiday, she'd asked if she could host the Silver Stone barbecue.

Ashton's seventeen-year-old nephew, Tucker, had already arrived for the summer. He raced up to meet Ashton with Luke and Walker Stone hard on his heels. The three were at the stage between being boys and becoming men, with awkwardly long arms and legs like unruly horses and muscle built from hard ranch labour beginning to show on their limbs and torsos.

"Uncle Ashton, we're going fishing after lunch. Okay if we ride to the falls?"

"Any chores left?" Ashton asked.

Tucker shook his head.

Luke and Walker glanced at each other.

Luke shrugged. "We're supposed to help clean up after the barbecue, but there's no use starting until everybody's gone. We figured we'd do it after supper. There'll be plenty of light still."

A crowd had gathered at the Stones' ranch house. The boys had a point; they'd taken a while to gather, and they'd take a while to disperse. Good food and good conversation always made for a relaxing event.

Ashton nodded his approval but left the boys with a

warning. "Take care of your horses before you come clean. No leaving them sweated up in the stalls."

"Yes, sir," three voices rang in unison, and then they were off, running and laughing and shoving at each other excitedly.

Ashton stopped to say hello to the Stones then caught Ginny in the middle of bringing out a huge bowl of salad. "You grow all that?"

She grinned. "Yes, Mr. Stewart. The best rabbit food you'll ever enjoy."

"That's saying something." He winked. "Good job."

"Thanks." She glanced around as if looking to see who might overhear. "Don't fight with Mrs. Fallen today, okay? Or my dad will end up lecturing us kids again about the proper way to treat others with respect, even when we don't see eye to eye."

Ashton barely stopped his laugh. "Sonora and I don't fight."

"You talk loudly, I know." She wrinkled her nose. "You've said that before. But every time you get together, you talk loudly. My mom tried calling your discussions *dedicated debating* to see if it stopped Dad."

"And?"

"He still lectured us." Ginny sighed. "It involved lots of puns he thought were funny."

Ashton wiped off his grin and laid a hand over his heart. "I swear Sonora and I will avoid disrupting the sanctity of your barbecue with anything that would cause your father to break out the dad jokes."

She eyed him suspiciously. "Mr. Stewart…"

"Means we'll behave." He leaned in as well. "I'll tell your dad you get one get-out-of-lecture-free card from me."

She shoved out her hand. "Deal."

Ashton was still chuckling when he bumped into Walter a few minutes later. "Your daughter is a hoot."

"Talented, smart, gorgeous," Walter agreed. "The cooking skills she gets from her mother."

Ashton snickered as he patted the other man on the shoulder then went to fill a plate with food.

He was done with lunch when he finally tracked down Sonora. She sat a little distance from the house, staring toward the mountains. The frown on her face was the one she got when she was irritated about something. Annoyed but wondering if she'd made a mistake.

They'd spent enough time together over the past few months that he'd started to sense her moods and read her expressions. She wasn't overall a tough nut to crack, though. Just like she spoke bluntly, she didn't tend to hide what she felt.

He settled into the lawn chair beside her and dipped his chin in greeting.

She glared at him, hard. "You know when I tell you I don't agree with you, it doesn't mean I don't like you."

Ashton blinked. Where the hell had that come from? "What do you think I am, twelve? I'm not a child. It takes more than a few words to get my nose out of joint."

"Well, apparently *other* people think I'm mean to you."

A blast of laughter rang out before he thought better of it. So both he *and* Sonora had been given a talking-to today.

At least he could easily reassure her on this charge. "You're honest. I like that far better than if you were fake nice. Also, you're blunt when you make your observations. You don't get cutting or cruel while disagreeing with someone."

Her disgruntled expression faded a little. "Telling you you're delusional isn't unkind?"

"Not the way you say it," he returned. Yep. There it was. Amusement once again sparked in her eyes. "As if you're delighted to have made the discovery and you're sure it might pass...if I'm lucky."

She snickered. "Exactly. I'm not insulting your intellect. Just your choices at times."

He considered then conceded the truth less flippantly. "Sometimes you make good points."

"Well, didn't that admission sound as if you swallowed a bowl full of nails?" Sonora patted his hand. "I do like to have my say, to offer my opinion, but I try to do it only when it's appropriate and to otherwise mind my own business. It's always the other person's decision what to do with the ideas I offer."

Ashton nodded slowly. "You don't expect people—*people* being me in this case—to cave to your every whim every time."

"I don't expect you to listen to me half the time," she joked back. "If you realize I'm brilliant even two of ten times, I feel I've saved you some trouble."

"Well, don't worry about it. I know you like me, and that's good enough for me. I'm glad we're friends.

"Friends who annoy each other?"

Ashton snorted. "Friends who keep each other on their toes. Expand each other's horizons."

"Oh, you're not the least bit likely to do that for me," Sonora said blandly. "Not unless your suggestions begin to improve."

"I told you to take up scrapbooking, didn't I? It's hugely popular right now."

"Cutting pieces of paper into smaller pieces of paper, only to put them back together into larger pieces of paper." She eyed him sternly. "And then you suggested quilting, which is the same thing, only with fabric."

"So how's your garden doing?" He poured himself a glass of water from the pitcher on the table beside her. Changing the topic seemed the wisest choice.

She described her latest project, and he paid attention even as his thoughts went in a happy direction.

He hadn't expected this.

After a few uncomfortable waves at the beginning, they had developed what he considered a very good friendship. Not that he and Sonora spent much time physically in the same location. He saw her once or twice a week when she came to borrow a horse or to visit with Deb Stone. He'd helped saddle her horse and occasionally joined her riding when she didn't have anyone to go with her. She didn't know the trails after all.

And he had gone over to her place a few times to discuss what to do with her land and then to oversee the prep and planting.

They'd somehow spent more time on the phone than he'd ever believed possible.

When they did get together, Ginny was right; he and Sonora debated and argued, always having a thoroughly good time doing it. It was too bad the people around them thought that meant something other than the truth.

He liked that he didn't have to pull his punches. With her, he could call a spade a spade. He could grumble and complain and yet stop whenever he wanted, and she didn't keep harping on the topic.

Curiosity struck. "Who was telling you to stop being mean to me?" he asked.

"No one."

He let out an exasperated sigh. "*Sonora*, we just held an entire conversation based on that topic."

"Oh, see they didn't tell me to *stop* being mean to you—they just said I *was* mean to you." She shrieked as he tossed his water at her, flying from her seat to a stop a few feet from the chairs. "Terrible man."

He stretched his arm a few times. "Sorry, involuntary reaction. Happens sometimes when cowboys get old."

She rolled her eyes toward the heavens, but she laughed. "First off, *again*, you're not old. And second, you're so full of bullshit."

"Language," he scolded. "Can't believe you're a grandma with the number of curses you drop."

Sonora settled back beside him. "Only around you, Ashton. Only around you."

This thing between them was something to be thankful for. Another friend his own age was good to have, but for that friend to be a woman with a bright mind and ceaseless energy?

Damn special.

Ashton leaned back in his chair and smiled harder as Sonora spoke animatedly, hands waving. No. He had nothing to complain about at all.

This was right. Here and now, this was right.

4

———

February, fourteen years ago

Icy fingers wrapped around Ashton's shoulders. He paused in the middle of raking at the hard-packed dirt of the stall, the cold surrounding him nowhere near the cold racking his gut.

The past forty-eight hours had been a nightmare. Even standing on the outskirts of the disaster, Ashton felt raked up one side and down the other by death's touch.

His friends were gone. A senseless car accident on wintry roads had taken the lives of Walter and Deb Stone and their friends the Hayeses.

The Stone family was now headed by twenty-four-year-old Caleb. Luke would turn twenty in a few days, and Walker was going on eighteen, which meant they were both old enough to take on more tasks and help keep things going. But Ginny was not yet sixteen, and Dusty was only eight.

Babies, all of them, in a moment like this.

Ashton wasn't worried about his job. He was needed at Silver Stone now more than ever. But the kids—goddamn, the *kids*. Their entire world had been turned upside down. How did they make it through this without breaking forever?

A soft sound, out of place and unexpected, caught his attention, and Ashton stopped to listen. It came again, and he propped the rake against the stall wall and quietly paced toward the noise.

In the far corner of the barn, hidden against one of the old-timer horses, Ashton's nephew, Tucker, stood weeping. The horse swayed slightly, the floorboards creaking, giving away their location.

With his face pressed to the gelding's neck, Tucker rocked in place as he mourned. Another person for whom the loss would feel unbearable. Tucker's relationship with Walter and Deb had been closer than the one he had with his own parents. Tucker had come to Silver Stone the instant he'd heard about the accident to be there for his friend Luke and for the others.

To be there to say his own farewells.

Ashton took a deep breath then stepped forward to wrap his arms around his nephew's shoulders.

Tucker turned into the embrace and squeezed tightly, no masculine pride holding him back. At nearly twenty, the young man unashamedly wept. "I can't—I can't believe they won't be back."

"I know." Ashton's words were gruff through a throat gone raw from shoving down his own pain.

He'd mourn later. For now, he needed to be strong.

Tucker breathed unsteadily, backing up as he wiped his eyes. "Sorry."

Ashton glared. No way would he accept that bullshit. "For what? For letting me see how much they meant to you? For mourning good people taken too soon? For hating that what we'd hoped to enjoy for years is gone in an instant?"

"You're right." His nephew nodded, his body tight. "It's unbelievable."

"Because we don't want it to be true. But it is." Ashton spoke softly, half to Tucker, half to himself. "It's not going to be easy, but we'll find a way to get through. One day at a time, okay?"

Tucker nodded. Sorrow darkened his eyes, his face drawn taut.

Ashton looped an arm around the young man's shoulder and guided him toward the door. "Get some fresh air. Walk in the sunshine then go find Luke. I'm sure he needs you."

His nephew slowly paced away, face lifted toward the sky as if trying to soak in some positive energy. Ashton didn't blame him one bit.

Ashton finished his task then took his own advice, walking outside until the tip of his nose tingled from the cold and his legs ached. He avoided the cookhouse, stopping briefly at the main Silver Stone ranch house to touch base with Caleb. It took a few minutes to reassure the young man that the ranch was under control and to discuss funeral plans for the next day.

By the time Ashton returned to his bunkhouse rooms, he was no longer cold physically, but the chill still held his heart. He ate a simple meal then sat on the couch and stared into the darkness.

Life turned on a dime. He knew that, but it wasn't supposed to take good people like the Stones. So many dreams were broken now. So many hearts.

He hung his head and cradled it in his hands.

The door to his bunkhouse burst open.

Ashton was on his feet a second later, an echo of terror from the accident's announcement a few days earlier ringing in his head far too loudly.

A second later, his heart kicked back into gear as Sonora stepped into view. She'd been out of town when it happened, and this was the first time he'd seen her since the horrid news had broken.

"Oh, Ashton. I'm so sorry." The words were gentle as she made her way quickly across the room to where he stood. She cupped his face, turning him toward her.

He couldn't speak. Not now.

She didn't seem to care. Instead, she wrapped her arms around him and held him tightly. Bodies close, hearts even closer.

The loss of his friends cut deep, and the only thing keeping him on his feet was the need to be there for the children. Willpower would have to get him through.

But in that moment, having Sonora brace him up turned the knot of hopelessness inside him the faintest hint brighter. Gave him the chance to let his pain out before it swamped him as well—

No, that wasn't right. He had to be strong. For everyone, even her. Damn if he'd do anything except soldier on.

He nodded, patting her back briefly before pulling free from her embrace. "Thanks. Poor kids. They've got so much on their plates right now, I'm amazed they're standing."

"It's not going to be easy days ahead. Not for anyone." She spoke softly, but her message was clear.

Ashton straightened. "I'll be there for them. Walter would want that. For me to be there for them to rely on, to guide them. To be strong."

Her expression hardened slightly. Her chin dipped, but even as she spoke, there was something in her eyes that warned him to be prepared.

"I hear what you're saying. I won't say you're wrong, but I will tell you this..." Her fingers tightened on his. "The children *will* be grateful you're there to help them deal with their loss. But Ashton, who's going to help you?"

That knot was back in his throat, and he didn't have an answer.

With the immeasurable strength that was so much a part of her, Sonora took over. She grabbed them both drinks then crowded him toward the couch. After resting the glasses on the table, she linked her fingers with his.

"Tell me something," she encouraged. "Share a moment you want to remember."

So many images flooded his mind. "The first time Walter and I worked together, he roped a calf that changed direction at the last second. It was the best damned thing I'd ever seen. Like magic." Ashton considered and then grinned. "A couple years later, he finally admitted it had been complete luck. He'd been stung by a wasp, and the shock made him release the rope early, accidentally catching the beast."

She shook her head, amused. "He probably kept his grin in place the entire time."

"Yup."

One story led to the next. A half hour later, they were in the middle of laughing together at a shared memory, a bright, sweet star shining in the darkness—

Sudden pain stabbed Ashton's heart. His laughter turned to a sob, and he wept as freely as Tucker had that morning.

Sonora cradled his head to her chest and held him. Silent yet strong.

They stayed that way for a good ten minutes as Ashton let out the sorrow that threatened to overwhelm him. Slowly, he came to a place where the hurt was still there but slightly more bearable.

He wiped himself up, considering what to say before he inadvertently copied Tucker's earlier mistake. "I won't cheapen that by apologizing."

Sonora shook her head. "Never. We're friends, and you should never apologize for showing your heart to a friend."

The room went quiet for a moment; then Ashton asked, "Will you come to the graveside with me? With the family?"

"I would be honoured."

Which was how Sonora ended up riding beside him the next afternoon as they joined the line of horses making a slow procession to the hillside location on Silver Stone land. The Hayes family had already been buried the day before in the community graveyard. This was the Stones' turn to say goodbye.

Ashton had come up to the ridge earlier with some of the hands. They'd used a backhoe to dig the graves, and that morning they'd already lowered the caskets into position.

Now Ashton stood with the Silver Stone children and their aunt and uncle, joining in as silent witnesses. Tucker and Sonora stood with the group as well, while Malachi Fields spoke the words for the funeral.

Caleb had asked for the ceremony to be as simple as possible for the sake of the younger kids. Malachi kept it brief; then each member of the family moved in turn to drop a handful of dirt over the coffins.

Luke and Walker paced beside each other, faces drawn with unhappiness. Ginny followed them, hand in hand with her best friend, Dare, both weeping silently, tears pouring down their cheeks.

Little Dusty held his brother Caleb's hand, squeezing dirt tightly in his other fist.

They stopped beside the graves. Dusty sniffed hard, shaking his head as he refused to let the dirt go.

Goddamn. Ashton glanced skyward, searching for wisdom. How could anyone explain to a kid that age there was no way to turn the clock back? No way to have his parents return.

Caleb scooped his little brother into his arms and held him close, whispering seriously.

Finally, Dusty nodded. He wiped at his eyes with the back

of his hand then turned and all but hurled the dirt over the graves before burying his face against Caleb's neck.

The family left, a slow, solemn procession, returning to their forever-changed home.

Ashton remained behind. He helped the men finish covering the graves, pausing to stare at the final resting place of his friends.

It had been too soon. Far, far too soon to have to say farewell. Still, he did it. Out loud, because it seemed the only way to be sure he also let go of the dirt.

"Goodbye. I promise I'll be here for them."

Turning, Ashton was shocked to discover Sonora had remained. She looked at him with those silvery-blue eyes, sadness and pride in their depths.

She gently touched his face. "Come on. Let's get you home."

5

Sonora's heart ached, but now it was her turn to give.

She guided Ashton off the hillside, taking charge because he needed her to. It wasn't only the winter chill that put that lost expression into Ashton's eyes. Simply taking him to his bunkhouse room wasn't the answer.

He needed a break from the pain. From the memories.

Sonora asked, though, to be sure. "Okay if we go to my place?"

A quick dip of his head was all the response she got, so she led him to her truck and drove the short distance to her home, pulling him behind her into the warmth of her house.

Ashton moved as if someone else were in control of his limbs. He shuffled to stand before the fireplace, staring wordlessly into the glass-fronted stove as she added wood until the flames licked over the fuel.

He wasn't going anywhere for a bit. Sonora dragged over a sturdy kitchen chair and pushed him into it.

She put on the kettle then silently sat beside him.

When he caught her fingers in his, Sonora sighed, wishing things could be different.

He snorted. "I'm not going to break apart, woman."

"Of course not." Sonora eyed him as haughtily as possible. "That would be too sensible."

The noise he made this time was bigger than a snort. His lips twisted slightly. "Thanks for being there."

No need to keep repeating polite inanities. Sonora lifted a hand to his cheek. "Warming up?"

The scruff on his jawline teased her palm.

Out of nowhere, unexpected and unasked, the urge to taste him struck.

She barely kept from jerking her hand away. What nonsense was this? This was Ashton. Her friend. Her very *platonic* friend...

A man grieving to his core.

She pressed her other hand to his face to stop from doing something inappropriate. This was a time for reflection and mourning.

But...Ashton didn't move. Not a single inch since she'd shifted into closer proximity. His gaze, that had been locked on her eyes, dipped to her mouth.

"*Sonora.*" Her name came out raw. Deep. Needy.

Sonora licked her lips. "Oh, dear."

His gaze flicked upward to meet hers again. "What?" he growled.

Inappropriate? Maybe—or maybe not. "I think I'm about to do something," Sonora warned. She hesitated then decided *to hell with it.* "No. I *know* I'm about to do something. Brace yourself..."

He opened his mouth, probably to complain, or scold, or do one of the dozen things typical between them.

Which meant that when she brought her mouth to his, the kiss went from what should have been an innocent brush of lips to something wildly intimate in seconds flat.

Their tongues made contact. A gentle tease growing more

insistent as they learned each other's taste. Learned how to angle properly to avoid bumping noses or any other awkward interruptions.

His hands slid onto her torso. The next moment, Ashton dragged her upward, and suddenly the entire front of her body was pressed to his firm angles and ridges and, dear Lord—

It was wonderful.

They might be mourning, but this was right. When death arrived on the scene, life shone in contrast like a bright spotlight. Life erased the darkness from the shadows. Eased sorrow from the core of humankind.

While death took, life gave.

Sonora threaded her fingers through his hair, stroking and caressing as if Ashton were some kind of big barn cat. His rough grumble of pleasure in response made her smile, the image of a cat only reinforced.

Ashton adjusted his stance until one thick thigh rested between her legs. The level of intimacy between them notched higher once again. The hard muscle of his leg pressed the sensitive nerves of her sex, and she gasped in pleasure. In need.

In *want*.

Aching, driving desire.

Forget platonic. She wanted this. She wanted *him*. She wanted to offer as well as take. In this moment, she wanted to brush away his sadness and *give*.

Thankfully, Ashton was fully on board with the idea as well. He worked her buttons, rough fingertips like erotic sandpaper causing shivers with every contact against her skin.

Frantically, she reached for his shirt. With fingers uncoordinated by lust, she jerked until she untucked the fabric from his jeans.

His skin was hot under her fingers and palms as she caressed past his waist and up the firm muscles of his back.

He paused in his own exploration to jerk his shirt over his

head. Then he reached for her and did the same, her blouse flying away to land somewhere.

Where exactly, Sonora didn't know or care. Because Ashton had undone the top button of his jeans and part of his zipper, and his naked abs and torso drew her forward as if she were a steel bar and he a magnet.

His expression, a hot, heavy-lidded gaze, swept over where she stood clad in her pants and bra.

"I want you naked," he growled.

"Eventually," she teased, stepping against him to stroke and caress, her fingers tracing every muscular inch. All the while they kissed. The heat between them was alive and wild.

A moan of pleasure escaped as he trailed his lips over her throat to the edge of her bra.

Skin supersensitive to the tracing of his tongue, Sonora gasped when he covered her nipple through the fabric and nipped lightly.

"Not going to let you boss me around when we're doing this, Sonora." He held her tightly, shoving aside her bra to get at naked skin.

She arched, straining closer even as she gave him sass. "Is that what you think? That you're the boss?"

He swept her into his arms, grinning as she clutched at his shoulders and held on tight. His strong steps carried them farther into the house and down the hall. "Here and now? Damn right, I am. You can pretend it's not what you want," he said the instant before he leaned over her and lowered his voice. "It would be a lie, though, and you don't lie."

The next second she flew. A squeal broke free as she bounced on her mattress, and before she could recover, he was there. Prowling over her like a cat again.

Had she thought him a barn cat? Hardly. A tiger, or a cougar, or a mountain lion maybe. Good thing she liked felines, no matter the size.

Ashton gazed down, his eyes drifting over her bared skin. "As I was saying, naked works better for me."

Sonora had to give the man credit. Seconds later, her bra was undone. Ashton peeled the remaining fabric from her body, leaving her without a stitch on.

His expression was somewhere between gloating and awed. "Damn, Sonora. I had no idea."

He settled between her legs, fingers tracing the lines of her tattoo.

She'd gotten the first part of it the summer after Greg had passed away, and since then she'd added more details every few years.

A simple wisteria vine swirled over her hip and up the side of her waist. Stylized leaves in varying shades of green had been stenciled on her skin for each of the people she'd loved over her lifetime. Tansy and roses in honour of two of her granddaughters. Ivy and fern branches woven in for the other two. Symbols for her daughter and son-in-law and others who'd made an impact on her life.

Ashton stroked a leaf, nodding in approval. "I see names in the vines."

"Family. Friends," Sonora told him. "They're always with me."

He pressed his lips to the crest of her hip bone, humming his approval. A second later he nipped, and examining her tattoo was pushed aside as heat rose.

"You good with this?" His voice had gone gruff again, his need clear in the tone and in the tightening grip of his fingers on her hips.

"Yes." Sonora curled upright, reaching for him.

He pressed a hand over her torso and pushed her back before dropping between her legs and rubbing his chin over her sex.

Sonora closed her eyes as he opened her with a gentle

touch and eased his mouth over her. Soft kisses, gentle licks, slowly growing harder and more insistent. By the time he slipped a finger into her, she was fighting for air and vibrating with need.

She threaded her fingers through his hair, gasping when he sucked and edged the fingertips inside her to exactly the right spot.

"There. More," she demanded.

His instant response was to double down until stars floated in front of her eyes and pleasure spiraled up and up and up—

Her orgasm broke. Body tightening around Ashton's fingers, Sonora moaned in satisfaction. It had been a long time since anyone other than herself had been involved in making her come.

But it wasn't enough. She tugged on his hair until he tilted his head back, grin flashing her way.

Cocky bastard. Well-deserved cockiness, to be sure.

"Get up here," she ordered.

"Yes, ma'am." He paused, hands on his jeans. "I don't have a condom."

"Good thing one of us is a Boy Scout." She rummaged in her side table and pulled one out.

He eyed the package briefly then covered himself, returning to her side. Slow, soft kisses resumed as he touched and moved her where he wanted. Sliding over her, the coarse hair on his thighs scratched hers as he pushed into position. The tip of his cock rocked through her wetness as he undulated his hips over and over.

When he adjusted the angle just enough to slip slightly deeper, she sucked in air.

Ashton slowed, withdrew, then rocked forward again. Small, teasing dips guided her desire back up. When he leaned up on one elbow and eased a hand between them to tease her clit, her core tightened, and the trickle of pleasure became a stream.

Sonora wrapped her legs around his thighs, sliding upward until her heels dug into his muscular ass. He moved faster, slow and soft forgotten as the heat between them roared like wildfire. Hot. Urgent, uncontrollable.

Driving deep now, Ashton held himself over her on both arms, gaze rolling over her breasts, her face, to the connection between them.

Fingernails biting into his shoulders, she hovered on the edge, waiting to go over one more time.

"Give it to me," he demanded. "You're so damn hot and wet around me. Fucking perfect."

The dirty words triggered her downfall. Sonora gasped as she came again, wrapping herself around him as he broke. His face twisted in ecstasy, eyes closed, lips parted as he groaned.

Time stood still. One quiet moment with no past, no future. Only pleasure and warmth and here and now.

Eventually he moved, twisting sideways to drop beside her on the bed. Her breathing was still uneven, and the room spun slightly. Their legs remained tangled, hands linked together.

Ashton's hot breath teased her skin. He freed one hand and brushed it up her body, smoothing over her neck to cup her cheek. He moved away briefly to deal with the condom then returned to her side.

The entire escapade had been unexpectedly wonderful. "Wow."

"Right?" His grin was definitely on the cocky side.

Then his expression shattered, sliding back to sadness and grief as he remembered. Sorrow rushed in like a wave and broke over them.

Sonora lifted a finger and all but shook it at him...and at herself, because for an instant, the same thoughts had hit her. "No."

She didn't have to say more before he pulled a face. "You're right. This was—" He paused, arching a brow. "Celebrating that we're not the ones under six feet of dirt right now sounds harsh, but it's also true."

"Do you really think Walter and Deb would want you to weep and cry? Or would they have been okay that you found a way to, as you said, celebrate life?" Sonora asked quietly.

To her astonishment, Ashton laughed. "Walter is probably cheering right now. He's been waiting for years for me to succumb to your charms."

Sonora rolled her eyes. "He was a terrible tease."

Ashton rolled her under him. While his eyes were lighter than they'd been before, they still held a note of concern. "He was right, though. We were inevitable. I guess we should talk about what comes next."

She liked the feel of him in her bed, heavy and in control, but she didn't think he was talking about them enjoying more sex. He had that *look*—the one that said she was about to dislike the turn in conversation.

She gave him the benefit of the doubt, though. "What do you mean, 'what comes next'?"

"We shouldn't rush things," Ashton said. "There'll be a lot going on at Silver Stone. I'll need to focus on that so I can guide Caleb, but we could plan a wedding for next summer—"

"Hold your damn horses." Somehow, she said it without shouting. Sonora was proud of her control. "Why on earth would we get married?"

He blinked. "Because—"

"And you need to reconsider quickly if the words *because we had sex* were about to come out of your mouth. This isn't the turn of the century, and I'm no sheltered miss." Sonora offered him a second chance, smiling as she caressed his cheek. "Marriage is something precious. It's a commitment and a vow between people who love each other. Sex is something completely different. Neither is more right or wrong, except for when people get the two mixed up."

Ashton held his tongue, but he frowned.

She stroked the furrow between his brows, smoothing it away. "Tonight was for both of us. A celebration of life, like you said. Of knowing it can be gone in an instant but for now, we're still here. We feel, we love, we care."

She maintained eye contact as he considered.

Sonora really hoped he figured this one out fast before she had to deck him.

IT WASN'T A LITERAL TWO-BY-FOUR, but Sonora's words were close to that figuratively. The truth struck hard and fast because she was right.

Being together after such a devastating loss had filled his soul and broken the ice surrounding his heart. But this hadn't been about starting a new path forward together. If he pushed the wrong way, the relationship between them could break. Could turn something beautiful and right into dust.

The days ahead were going to drain him. Of time, of energy, of strength. Going forward, Ashton imagined he'd be running at times on sheer willpower. It wasn't the time to start a new relationship.

He didn't need a lover. More than ever, he needed a friend.

For a split second, something deep inside fought to complain before he shoved it away. It might not be what he really wanted, but he was smart enough to listen to reason.

Ashton rolled to his side and pulled her against him and held on tight. Not speaking, not doing anything except telling his brain she was right, and this—*they*—needed to stay the same.

There would be enough changes in the world in the days to come.

Sonora remained stiff at first, but the longer he held her, the more her tension eased. Once again, giving to him.

It was time to accept the wisdom of her words, not just for this moment together but in knowing it wasn't a forever thing.

"Friends?" He said it softly. Offered it, really, like a token in the hopes she'd return it to him.

She twisted until she found his hand, lifted it to her lips, and kissed his knuckles gently. "Friends." Her face was smooth again. No sign of worry or fear or sadness. Just solid confidence. "We can do this, Ashton. We just need to go back to what we do best."

"Arguing?" he suggested. Although, to be truthful, the sex had been great as well.

Her eyes lit up. "Is it terrible that I enjoy seeing everyone around us imagine us to be archenemies? I mean, you do annoy the hell out of me at times, don't get me wrong."

"But sometimes it's fun to play it up a little just to pull their chains. Get a reaction from them." Ashton leaned his head closer. "Although I'd never admit to such a thing."

She grinned. "Ha. It being true and actually admitting it are two vastly different things, Ashton Stewart."

There she was. Once again his co-conspirator. An understanding heart who'd helped ease his pain and soothed away some of his fears during the darkest of times.

Ashton took a deep breath. "It's going to be tough. The days ahead."

She nodded. "They will be. But they'll be easier with friends by your side."

The fact they were still naked under the covers suddenly didn't matter. The sex they'd shared was still between them, but this other sensation was somehow more. Bigger. Something Ashton didn't want to mess up because it was important.

But still, he held her for a little longer, the two of them quiet as the house creaked and settled into the darkness of night.

Friends. For now. Maybe for always.

Ashton listened to her quiet heartbeat and mourned.

55

THE GHOSTS OF CHRISTMAS PAST

December, two years ago

Snow was falling again.

Sonora stared out her living room window at the large fluffy flakes magically appearing from a nearly cloudless sky, and she wondered how true the *storm of the decade* rumours were.

She'd been in Heart Falls for sixteen years now and had spoken with enough friends who'd lived here all their lives to know the seasons followed rhythms. A hard winter every six or seven years, with something spectacular every ten.

It was time for another environmental extravaganza.

At the edge of her line of vision, a truck paused out on the highway then turned toward her house. It was nearly at the house when she recognized it was Ashton.

Sonora sighed. Another rhythm, only this one was less amusing to solve than the snow-or-no-snow conundrum.

Or perhaps she should call the man's presence a drumbeat.

A faint, ever-present noise in the background that only got louder the closer he got.

Like the local weather, Sonora had learned a lot about Ashton over the past years. Their relationship had ebbed and flowed, sometimes closer, sometimes drifting apart with longer spaces between interactions. The past nine months had been extra busy, especially after she impulsively started an animal rescue in her barn with help from the community.

And Ashton, she supposed.

Always Ashton.

For some strange reason, something had begun to change. And along with the changes came a growing urge to speak about the twisting ideas in her head and heart that were no longer so clear.

You're supposed to be friends.

The thought was hers, but she heard the words in Greg's voice. The ghost of her husband's voice still echoed in her brain at the most inconvenient times.

"We are. Grumbly friends," Sonora insisted, watching as Ashton drove toward his favourite spot to the side of her house instead of in front where everyone else stopped. "Have been forever by this point in our lives. And that's just fine with me."

Bullshit.

"It is not bullshit. I have no desire for us to become anything more than friends."

Lying doesn't suit you, Sonora Fallen. Neither does cowardice. Sixteen years is long enough that you should be able to admit you admire the man. Plus, you're lonely. You would not mind him in your bed.

And maybe more.

"Shut up, Greg." Sonora's sense of humour was running low today. She wasn't ready to deal with ghosts calling her out or offering up ideas that were nothing but trouble.

Trouble because anything other than friendship was not what she and Ashton agreed to after the one time.

Funny how she could see that phrase written in her head. Capitals and italics. *The One Time.*

Their single sexual escapade had become a daydream she'd fall into, details blurring as more and more time passed. Like a special feature that had only ever been performed once, live, before the days of video, streaming media, and instant replays.

She wasn't sure when exactly the other changes had begun. They were so used to simply being themselves around others, sniping and poking, that no one seemed to believe it was even possible for them to want more.

And more is what you want. Admit it...

"Fine. Damn you, Greg. I do want more."

Sonora still wasn't sure *what* more she wanted, but the certainty of not wanting to continue what she and Ashton had been doing for years left her teetering on unfamiliar ground.

The doorbell rang.

She stepped forward slowly, summoning her control until she was able to offer a bright smile to the man standing on her front stoop. "Ashton. What a surprise."

"Hardly." He pushed past her, tugging the door closed behind him to stop the warm air from escaping. "You go to town every Saturday."

For once he managed to confound her. "So?"

He gestured outside. "There's a storm coming. I figured you're too stubborn to stay home like you should. I'll drive you."

Again with the great idea offered in a dictatorial manner. It appeared *some* things never changed.

Sonora leaned toward the window. She ignored the light snow and peered pointedly at the huge patch of bright blue sky. "Definitely looks like trouble. I'm sure I can't be trusted to drive in these conditions. So glad you're here to stop poor little me from making bad choices."

He sighed. "Sorry. I did it again, didn't I?"

She patted his shoulder on her way to where her boots and purse rested. "You did, but your heart is in the right place. Give me a minute, and I'll be ready to go."

Coat, boots, scarf, and mitts later, Sonora reached for the large wicker basket full of things she wanted to drop off at her daughter's.

"Let me carry that for you," Ashton offered.

"You'd think I was some kind of delicate flower the way you baby me at times," she scolded softly, but she pulled the door open for him and let him go first.

"Not delicate. Jeez, woman, let a man treat you with respect without giving him sass." He not only carried the basket, he offered his hand and helped her down the stairs and through the snow to the passenger side of the truck. "Don't open that."

Sonora jerked to a stop, hand hovering over the door handle.

While she waited, he hauled open the back door and placed her basket on the seat then hurried forward to open her door.

"Really?" she asked in disbelief when he bent and cupped his hands the way he did when assisting her to mount her horse.

"It's a long way up, and you're short," he said blandly. When she rolled her eyes at him, he shook his head but stayed where he was. "Stubborn."

"We've had this conversation before," she pointed out. "Your truck is not my horse. I can get into the cab on my own, just like I'm capable of carrying my own things."

"Face it. If I *hadn't* offered to carry the basket, you'd have called me a caveman and a lout and then ordered me to pick it up for you."

She laughed as she leaned closer, putting them eye to eye.

Smiling widely, she all but bumped noses with him. "You. Are. Correct."

She'd meant it as a tease. Had meant to simply poke him a little, but being this close, the scent of him surrounding her—dear Lord, what was wrong? All of a sudden, she was feverish. On fire from the inside out.

And whatever she had, he'd been struck with as well. His tanned cheeks flushed, eyes bright.

They both backed up rapidly.

Sonora reached for the oh-shit handle to haul herself upward, half flying to the bench when Ashton caught her by the hips and lifted.

She had the length of time it took for him to pace around the truck to get her heart rate to drop to near normal.

What had *that* been? Obviously, she was feeling confused these days, but that—

One more deep inhale from Sonora before he settled beside her and started the engine. "Where are you headed?" he asked with a growl.

She clutched at the bit of normalcy. "Sophie's. And perhaps to Buns and Roses. I haven't seen Rose or Tansy for over a week."

"Really? You usually stop in there every other day."

"Just been busy." She had been, sort of, but the actual truth was a confession Sonora would not make to Ashton.

She'd accidentally backed her truck into a tree last Sunday and wasn't sure it was still road legal. She hadn't gotten around to calling the shop to fix the bumper, mostly because she was too embarrassed by the whole thing.

Good thing Ashton had shown up when he did, or she'd have been forced to confess her mistake to her son-in-law when she pulled into his driveway this morning and asked for help.

"I can drop you at your daughter's, but I need to stop at the mercantile first."

"Of course. It's on the way." Sonora examined at the sky. "It's far too pretty out for what they're talking about on the news."

"Who knows what we'll truly end up with." He flashed a smile her way. "I'm just grateful we live in Alberta. My brother called this morning and said Winnipeg is an icebox. Minus forty, with colder temperatures expected tomorrow."

Sonora shivered, a full-body experience. "Nasty."

"Yup."

She twisted until she faced him. "How is your brother?"

Ashton sighed. "Miserable. Not that he ever does anything to change things, so he must be happy about it in some twisted way."

Over the years, Ashton had shared about the odd relationship his brother and his wife had. Their marriage had never made sense to Sonora. It seemed more a business relationship than two people in love. "He and his wife still at the university?"

"I think they'll be buried in the university research library," Ashton offered. He went quiet for a bit then shook his head as if getting rid of a nasty thought. He glanced her way and changed the topic completely. "You look good today."

Sonora blinked. "Thank you?"

He snorted. "Way to take a compliment."

"I'd thought I'd used up my quota of compliments for the year already."

His lips twitched. "Am I that terrible about saying nice things to you?"

She shrugged. "Don't know why you'd need to say nice things to me more often than you do. I was joking. Don't worry about it."

"But you do look good," he said softly, his gaze locked on the road in front of them as they neared the first shops of Heart Falls. "And I noticed."

The tone of his voice was different, and a shiver raced over her. This one completely different than a response to cold temperatures. This was about heat, and need, and—

Friends, remember?

But when Ashton pulled the truck off the road and parked it to the side of the mercantile, that *something* in the air was back.

He turned off the engine but held on to the wheel for a long moment.

Sonora eyed him. "You okay?"

He blew out a breath as if preparing for a difficult task. He faced her, and his expression—

Dear Lord. That was not the expression of a friend. Good, caring, grumbly friends didn't look at each other as if they were starving.

"I always notice."

Sonora's heart raced. "Ashton?"

He moved decisively. A moment later, he had a hand curled around her neck as he tugged her toward him.

"Kiss me back," he ordered.

His lips were on hers before she could say *okay*.

The memory of his mouth that she'd replayed over and over in her mind had obviously faded in intensity over the years, because this was far more spectacular. Lips firm, hands controlling, Ashton took her, demanding a response with teeth and tongue and urgent desire.

The hand around her neck stayed securely in place, but the other slipped down her coat's zipper and then around her waist, tugging her entire body across the center of the bench seat. Then he cupped her over her sweater, one big hand cradling her breast as if he owned her.

Impossible. This was utterly impossible. Sonora could not fathom how they'd gone from talking about winter weather to kissing each other with such passion that her body was a full toes-to-the-top-of-her-head tingle of pleasure.

Impossible, but who cared? It was good. Very, *very* good.

Sudden space opened between them as he all but shoved her away. "No. We're not doing this. It's all wrong."

Breathing was still difficult, as was thinking. In under a minute, he'd somehow stolen her ability to concentrate. Amused, she finally found her words. "We seemed to be doing it just fine. In fact—"

In for a penny at this point. Sonora adjusted position before climbing onto the bench seat to face him. One hand to his chest, she leaned in slowly.

His pupils were huge, chest rocking with each deep breath he took. His hands landed on her hips, strong fingers squeezing tight and easing her even closer.

He tilted his head and took her lips on the next move, and Sonora held on for the ride.

Wrong? No, this was perfectly right.

A quick move, and he'd slipped her shirt free from her pants and pressed his fingers to her bare skin. He traced gentle circles that tickled even as they ignited fire all over her.

He groaned and deepened the kiss, and she was ready to haul him over her on the front seat, damn the consequences.

The next second she was airborne, lifted from his lap and dropped on the bench seat.

She'd barely caught her balance when icy cold swirled around her. He had shoved his door open, fleeing from the truck. He jammed his hat in place as his gaze shot to meet hers. Panting for breath, eyes on fire, he looked one step away from ravishing her.

Maybe she should have been annoyed that his kiss had come out of the blue, but instead she felt a distinct lack of displeasure at his odd behaviour. She wanted him, wanted this, and, as her granddaughters would say, stopping sucked.

He didn't speak. Just stared at her.

Sonora pulled herself together a little. "We should talk about this."

Ashton jabbed a finger in her direction, still not saying anything.

She raised a brow. Waited.

"Sit. Stay," he growled.

He slammed the door behind him, puffs of snow swirling into the air like miniature ice pixies roused to battle.

She stared after him. Confused. Shocked.

He'd...left? Kissed her and then left.

Without a word. Without—well, no shouting or complaining or anything typical like that. Just a very annoying Ashton Stewart in bossy mode. Sit, stay. As if she were a freaking *dog*.

He'd *left*.

Temper rising, Sonora glared out the window at the mercantile to the right of the truck. Ashton had already gone in, which was good, because she would have been tempted to jump out and beam a snowball at him.

She folded her arms over her chest and allowed anger to flare hot and bright. No use wasting a good mad on a cold day. Fury got the blood pumping and all the rest of it.

If *she'd* kissed him out of the blue—forced *him*—she could understand his reaction better. Or if she'd had any inkling that he'd decided being kissed by her was so repugnant, she would have stopped instantly.

Yes, it had been an impulsive move, but he'd kissed her first. What. The. *Hell*.

She glanced out the window then, too restless to sit and with zero interest in obeying his order to wait like a good puppy, Sonora zipped up her coat.

Ignoring the basket in the backseat for now, she slipped out of the truck, squared her shoulders, and headed into town.

6

———

$\mathcal{A}$shton stood in line behind the counter, waiting his turn. He all but itched to abandon his task, march back to the truck, and start that talk Sonora had suggested. Talk, shout, whichever it took.

But that would require admitting he didn't have a clue what had been in his head a few minutes ago.

Dammit, he'd kissed her. *Groped* her. Hell, if they hadn't been parked right out in front of God and everyone, he'd have been tempted to strip her down and take her right on the seat of his truck.

Ashton scrubbed his hand over his face and fought for control. Kissing Sonora hadn't been a possibility for years except in his damn dreams. Why, now, had he lost it?

"I know, but what choice do I have?"

Oh.

Oh shit.

The comment from the conversation with his brother that morning came back in full force, echoing in his brain, and Ashton was tossed back in time like a fish on a line.

They'd been talking about the upcoming holiday season.

Not that there were any plans to actually get together for a gathering, not in their family. Ashton still liked to keep in touch for his nephew's sake, if nothing else…

~

"ALONG WITH THE usual faculty parties, we'll be hosting our annual Christmas events. This coming Friday night, Lynn's philharmonic association will be at the house." Steve sighed heavily. "Of course, she somehow booked it for the same night I planned our bridge-club formal."

"So which is it? Bridge or music?"

Steve snorted. "Saying things like that makes it clear you've never been married. Unless I wanted to deal with a moping woman for the entire month, it had to be music. I switched bridge to Sunday. Which meant *she* had to move the alumni dinner. It's so annoying to have to keep adjusting things. Lynn should be more careful."

"Didn't you double book at Thanksgiving? And Lynn had to rearrange things last minute?"

"Well, perhaps. But that was ages ago. I really feel our calendar would be better served by following my plans, not hers. But such is life."

"You two make my brain ache," Ashton said.

Really, Steve's passive-aggressive relationship with his wife made no one happy. The two of them didn't outright fight. They didn't cheat. They were outwardly ever so polite and considerate as they continually compromised their way into positions where they both ended up miserable. It had always been this way, but over the past years, it had only gotten worse.

As usual, the discussion with his brother triggered all the wrong reactions. Ashton knew he should keep his mouth shut.

But he couldn't.

"One or the other of you always being miserable is a terrible decision," he pointed out.

"I know, but what choice do I have?"

Choice? Ashton knew the answer to that one. "You could do something that makes you both happy for once in your damn lives."

"Well, when you take your own advice, I'll look you up." Steve offered a righteous snort then disconnected the call.

That was bullshit right there. Ashton *was* happy. He had a great job, wonderful people to work with, and good friends, including Sonora. The woman was a beautiful constant in his world. Steadfast and always entertaining, with their never-ending retorts and debates to keep him on his toes.

Sexy as sin as well.

Ashton froze. No. That was a path he was not allowed to go down...

~

"NEXT."

At the bored call from the clerk, Ashton jerked from his memories to the here and now as he made his way to the front counter. "Pickup for Silver Stone."

"Right away, Mr. Stewart." The man behind the counter turned and marched into the stacks, leaving Ashton with the fading memory of his morning and the growing realization of exactly what had caused his brain to misfire in the truck.

Witnessing the miserable life Steve and Lynn had created had influenced Ashton's choices in many ways over the years. Made him swear *he* was never getting married. Made him realize it was more valuable to focus his attention on his relationship with his nephew Tucker than to attempt to build anything with his brother.

But the dominant lightning bolt of this particular morning

had been finally acknowledging the terrible truth Ashton had deliberately shoved into a small box for years.

Kissing Sonora was definitely a choice he wanted to make.

After all this time of being friends, he wanted Sonora Fallen with something close to an addictive need. That didn't excuse his actions a few minutes ago in the truck, but it sure the hell explained it.

His brain might know jumping the woman wasn't a logical plan, but his instincts were full speed ahead.

What would make him truly happy? To have Sonora Fallen in his life, and specifically in his bed, full time, no questions asked. He didn't need a wife. He'd happily make them both hear bells ring on a regular basis without a more formal arrangement.

It was a long way from where his head had been the last and only time they'd tangled.

Perhaps even an old dog could learn new tricks.

That had been tangling his thoughts en route to pick her up today. How to broach the subject when them being a *them* hadn't been a possibility for longer than a decade.

Part of him knew any changes in their relationship would need to be eased into place. Even small things, like complimenting her on how pretty she looked—that was something he rarely did.

Mostly because looking too hard meant he ended up back at his place, dealing with himself or taking cold showers as fantasies about Sonora in his bed flashed in too-vivid detail in his brain.

No. Kissing Sonora had been a breakdown in control and showed a terrible lack of planning—

But he didn't really regret it. How could he regret one of the best moments of his life? Dear Lord, the woman tasted like sin.

The beam of sunshine on the floor by his feet vanished between one moment and the next. Ashton peered out the window at the storm clouds rushing overhead. The forecasted storm had arrived.

His phone buzzed.

He hauled it out before staring in confusion at the text from Sonora.

Sonora: *Do you know where the holiday star Gary Silver made went? It would have been taken home from the church in January two years ago or so, possibly by a United Church member. I'm certain all the pieces I knew about are accounted for.*

What was she going on about?

Also, *the hell*? Here he was, stewing about the fact he'd kissed her, certain she was plotting ways to detach and fry his balls. But instead of being tied up in mental knots like he was, she was daydreaming about holiday decorations?

"Troubles?" the guy behind the counter asked.

Ashton blinked.

The man gestured at Ashton's phone. "Looks as if you're ready to tell someone to take a hike."

Ashton shoved the contraption in his pocket. "Frustrating things. Thought they were supposed to be for our convenience."

"Sometimes it's best to ignore them completely," the other man suggested, pushing forward a large package. "Unless it's for work or an emergency, there's nothing people need to know this instant that can't wait until they see you in person."

At a moment like this, Ashton fully agreed. Although the chances of discussing Christmas decorations when he saw Sonora next was low. He'd prefer to kiss her until she couldn't see straight. Just to make certain she was as tied up inside as he was.

Kissing her. *Hell.* He needed to get his act together and

quickly. He'd basically blown his advantage by showing his cards too soon.

Still, Sonora was a mostly reasonable woman. Perhaps all it would take was one honest conversation between them.

It was time to choose something that could make them both happy. He was sure of it.

He pushed out of the shop doors into the teeth of an icy wind. The storm could work to his advantage. He'd sweet-talk her into visiting her daughter another time. Instead, he'd take Sonora home then offer his revised relationship plan.

Happy with his scheme, Ashton pulled open the truck door. "How about we head home before—"

Sonora was gone.

Un-fucking-believable. He shoved the box onto the backseat, noted her basket was still there, then took a quick walk around the vehicle.

The wind had already begun to fill in her footprints, but she'd clearly gotten out and walked farther into town.

One good thing about living in a small town was that Ashton pretty much knew where she'd gone. He raced the truck down the highway, slamming to a stop in front of Buns and Roses coffee shop.

The bitter cold wind wrapped around him as he crossed the short distance to the front door, his anger rising hard and fast. She could have been caught out in that blast. Had she even considered that before taking off so foolishly?

He jerked open the café door and immediately spotted her. Sonora sat beside Brooke, the daughter of his best friend, Gary Silver. The two women looked cozy and comfortable, coffee cups in hand, plates with chocolate on the table before them.

The rush of relief only made his anger flare brighter, and he marched to their side.

Somehow he managed to offer a moderately friendly chin

dip to Brooke before glaring daggers at Sonora. "Are you out of your mind, woman?"

Sonora calmly returned his stony stare before she deliberately glanced away and sipped her coffee. "Last time I checked, no."

Ashton dropped into the empty third chair at the table. Ignoring everyone but Sonora, he spoke firmly, not even caring that his annoyance was clear in his voice. "When I offer to drive you to town, I expect you to stay put and let me drive you to all your destinations."

"I'm not a dog you can order to sit and stay, Ashton. If you feel the need to practice your canine training, drop by the animal shelter." Her bright eyes narrowed. "Or maybe not. You'd just get them all riled up and then leave."

He stiffened. That was a sharp, specific blow. Which meant she hadn't been completely unaffected by the kiss after all.

Across from him, Brooke sipped her coffee, eyeing him and Sonora with a great deal of interest. The younger woman didn't say anything, but her lips betrayed a hint of amusement before she pulled herself under control and pretended to be distracted by the treat on her plate.

He was about to say something else to Sonora when the wind gusted against the front window hard enough to rattle the double-paned glass, and the snow that had been threatening slammed into the building, seemingly out of nowhere.

The weather had officially turned. The forecasted winter storm had arrived, even wilder and more violent than expected.

"Wow. That's not looking very friendly." Brooke pushed back from the table to check out the huge front window. Whiteness blurred the buildings across the street.

"That's why I didn't want you wandering off," he told Sonora. Damn, he was all but growling at her. He deliberately lowered his voice, checking Sonora over with concern. "You know in this territory the storms sneak up quick. What if you'd still been walking when that hit?"

"I would have walked faster." But Sonora glanced past him and out the window, and her flushed cheeks paled.

The sight of her fear undid him, and he eased off. He wasn't about to fight her. Not here. They might have had fun in the past waging mock battles in public, but her fear and his anger were too real and raw to be displayed for entertainment's sake.

Instead, Ashton put two and two together then turned to Brooke. "I assume you're the one asking about the star?"

"Mack and I, yes. Do you know where it is?"

Ashton rubbed his jaw. His best friend ran the local mechanic shop with Brooke's help. Gary had helped Silver Stone ranch and others over the years, but only a few places would have used his skills with a welder. The list of people who would have stepped up when something large needed to be stored wasn't too long. "Maybe. I need to make a couple calls, but if I find it, I'll give you a shout."

"Don't mention this to Dad," she asked. "We're trying to make it a surprise."

Ashton assumed *we* meant her and Mack.

Mack, Brooke's boyfriend, was a local firefighter and a good man. Solid. But fathers didn't always like change when it was happening under their noses, and so far, Gary had held back from approving of the relationship.

Seemed the kids were trying to do something special for the holidays. A little late, considering it was already the twenty-first, but still.

Ashton nodded then glanced between Sonora and Brooke. "You ladies go ahead and take your time. I'll drive you both where you're going when you're done."

Sonora pressed her lips together, but she didn't complain.

Brooke didn't either—and within minutes the three of them were bundled up and in the truck, headed for the car shop.

Ashton pulled to a stop as close to the doors as he could. "Say hi to your dad for me," he said.

"I will. Call him if you have time. He was talking about trying for an evening at Rough Cut for beers and burgers."

"Will do."

Brooke opened and closed the door as quickly as possible, but the cab was still filled with icy coldness before she vanished into the shop.

Or maybe that was the chill radiating off Sonora.

Ashton turned the truck out of the parking lot. "We—"

"You are an ass." Sonora said it clearly then smiled sweetly. "What were you about to say?"

He didn't know if he should laugh or just shake his head. "Should I still drop you at your daughter's, or do I dare make a different suggestion?"

"You've got more ideas other than *sit, stay*? I'm all aquiver to hear them."

Yeah, he wasn't going to live that comment down any time soon. "Come to my place."

Sonora shook her head. "Take me home and we'll talk there. I don't feel like explaining the bloodstains on your bunkhouse floor to the Stone family if things get out of hand."

He snorted, turning the correct direction to follow her lead. "You think our discussion is going to get violent?"

"I'm not sure. You might be safe now that I've had time to reconsider." She leaned forward and peered at the clouds roiling overhead. "It really is nasty out there."

They sat in silence for the rest of the trip.

At the house, Sonora slipped out of the cab before Ashton could come around to help her. She opened the rarely used back door since it was closer, and he followed her in as quickly as possible.

The door closed behind them, and the shriek of the wind

was suddenly cut off, leaving the quiet of the house loud in his ears.

She shrugged out of her coat, slipped off her boots, then took all of two steps into the living room before turning to face him with her arms folded over her chest and one brow raised high.

He hung up his own things as he waited for her to give him hell. Waited for her to ask if he'd been drunk, or high, or simply pulling her chain.

But she just stood there, the silence growing like a living thing.

Ashton stepped closer, planning to head around her to the kitchen. He'd put on the kettle so they could make a pot of tea, one of Sonora's ever-present rituals. Then, once they both had something to do with their hands, he'd make it clear he'd been none of those things—drunk, high, or kidding.

But Sonora blocked his path. She lifted her chin, gaze fixed on his. "Talk."

"Right here?" Unable to resist, he lifted a hand, stroking back a lock of hair that had fallen from her ponytail.

"Right here," she insisted. Then her gaze narrowed, and her expression grew dangerous. "Unless you want to hold the discussion in my bedroom."

7

———

Getting older had done nothing but increase the odds that she would say exactly what was on her mind. Ashton's shocked expression proved being plainspoken was good for the amusement factor if nothing else.

He blinked then coughed, deliberately stepping around her. "I'll go put on the kettle."

"Which means no to the bedroom. Good to know. Life is so much easier when all the expectations are clear."

Ashton ignored her, shoving the kettle under the tap with more energy than required. "Going to be one hell of a conversation," he muttered.

"That was one hell of a curveball you threw me earlier," Sonora pointed out. "Why should the ensuing conversation be any less difficult?"

She held her tongue as she joined him in the kitchen. Between searching the refrigerator and digging into the cupboard, by the time he'd gathered the cups and had the kettle turned on, she had a plate with cookies and squares on the table. From habit more than the need for treats.

She sat in her usual spot, where the wonderful view of the

world outside her house always mesmerized her. Today it should have been even more so because of the storm raging across the landscape. But instead of staring at the snow whipping past as if in a frenzied disaster movie, she deliberately examined Ashton.

He adjusted the kettle then pulled over the sugar and honey pots. He twisted the cups he'd already placed on the counter, pushing them back slightly before nudging them an inch forward. He grabbed her washcloth from the sink and wiped everything down despite the fact there was zero chance anything was remotely dirty at this point in his venture.

When he adjusted the cups yet another time, she realized what was going on. Ashton Stewart was fidgeting. He was nervous, and that unusual fact was so charming that her lingering frustration eased.

Don't go easy on the guy just because you think he's cute.

Do you have to show up right when the situation is most delicate? she demanded of the ghost in her mind. *I'm not planning on going easy on him either,* she informed Greg.

But you do think he's cute.

Shut up, Greg.

Anyone analyzing her psyche at that moment would have needed a bottle of vodka and a year's worth of therapy.

By some unspoken agreement, Sonora and Ashton waited until the tea was ready and they were both seated comfortably at the table before speaking. It could've been one of a million times that they'd shared a moment like this over the years, except for how the butterflies in her belly said it was totally different.

Ashton wrapped both hands around his cup as if it were anchoring him to the ground, but he lifted his gaze and met hers firmly. "I won't apologize for kissing you."

She raised a brow. "Did I ask you to?"

He sighed heavily, shoulders drooping. "No, but you should have. It wasn't fair of me."

"What wasn't fair was kissing me then running away," Sonora said deliberately. "But neither of those things annoyed me as much as you ordering me around. Ashton, we've covered that topic *repeatedly* over the years. I'd hoped by now it had finally sunk in. I'm not your dog."

"You aren't," he agreed. His lips twitched. "Beauty is far better trained and actually listens to me."

Dear Lord. By some miracle, she kept from laughing out loud. His bad habits didn't need to be encouraged.

Focusing, Sonora rested her elbows on the table. "You should apologize for telling me to sit."

"I didn't want you to take off on me," he complained.

"And look how well that turned out," she snapped. An exasperated sigh escaped, but she got her tone back to civilized and calm. "Don't order me around. *Ask*."

"I know. You're right." He frowned at his teacup. "I'm sorry."

She waited.

He snorted. "I'm sorry for bossing you around instead of asking."

"Thank you." Sonora lowered her own cup and folded her hands together. It was her turn to be nervous. "Ashton, may I ask you something?"

"Of course."

She looked around the room at all her comfortable, familiar things. At the home that she'd built in this place that had come to mean so much to her.

It had been a process, and the man opposite her had been a part of that growth. He'd always been willing to help. Always been somewhere on the edges of what she was learning.

Maybe it was time to nudge him nearer to the center.

Sonora took a deep breath. "What would you think about us becoming...closer?"

He froze in place. "Why are you being less than blunt for the first time in your life? What does *closer* mean?"

Terrifying how direct that was. "I'm not sure," she admitted. "We're friends. I know that. And I care deeply about you."

"I care about you too," Ashton responded immediately.

"Yet you kissed me," Sonora said, raising a brow. "You never kiss me. Except on the cheek when it's a holiday gathering."

He nodded slowly. "May I ask *you* something?"

She snorted. "Listen to us. Of course you can. Let's just drop the awkward polite behaviour and have a typical Sonora/Ashton conversation."

"Fine. You kissed me back," Ashton said. He grinned. "Enthusiastically."

"It was entertaining," she started before shaking her head. "No. No teasing right now. Just truth. I did kiss you back. I liked it, and I was very willing to do more than kiss."

He frowned. "Was? You're not anymore?"

She raised a hand. "Semantics, that's all. I'm interested in things that I wasn't interested in before, but I don't know if any of those ideas fit with *us*, with who we've become over the years. I'm not willing to break a good friendship over the fact you have been the star in my dirty daydreams for far too long now."

Ashton's jaw hung open.

It felt good to finally give in to her laughter. "Clear enough?"

He nodded, eyes brightening. "Thank goodness for plainspoken women." He pushed aside the teacups and caught her fingers in his. "To answer your earlier question: Would I like to get closer? We're already friends. I care about you and want the best for you. I'd also like to have you under me, screaming my name because you're coming so hard around my cock that you're seeing stars."

Oh. *Oh...*

Sonora nodded slowly. "And that's plainspoken on your part."

"We do plainspoken well." Ashton stroked his thumb across her knuckles in a gentle caress. "Do you want us to start dating? Is the idea to go out for dinners and movies and the rest of it?"

Dating at sixty? She shook her head slowly. "That seems like a lot of work when we could simply move to the screaming-hot-sex part."

Ashton paused. "I don't want you to feel as if you're being used."

"There is nothing 'used' about two friends deciding to share something enjoyable." Sonora shrugged. "I have opinions about sex."

"I've noticed." Ashton winked, though. "It doesn't require marriage."

She laughed. "You were so cute that night. But obviously what I said sank in."

He nodded. "It did. And you're right; it's good for us to make the rules around this potential new thing between us crystal clear. Tell me again how this works in your brain."

Sonora paused to make sure the words of what she believed came out correctly. "Marriage is for love. When people feel committed at a heart level, that's the time to book the church and say *I do*."

Ashton stilled. "I care about you, Sonora, but I'm not the marrying type. I don't...love you...like that."

"Which is fine," she assured him. "I care about you as well, deeply. But I'm not looking for a ring and a church. I'm interested in sex, which is still a very big deal, just in different ways."

"Go on."

This part she'd considered often over the past weeks. "Sex is still a commitment. It's caring in a physical way and sharing joy that turns into pleasure for all parties involved."

"All *parties*?" Ashton frowned.

She waved his comment off. "Only two people in the bed for me, but I try to be inclusive in my wording these days. I have grandkids, and I have no idea who they'll get involved with in the future."

He shook his head. "Sticking to the here and now, are you saying you want to add sex to our relationship?"

"Committed sex. Only-you-with-only-me sex. No dating, no change of our relationship otherwise. Also, I don't think anyone else needs to know anything has changed. We've always spent time together. Always enjoyed the occasional outing but as friends. We'll just keep it at that."

"Agreed."

Sonora glanced around her home, the place she'd worked so hard to make hers, and she wasn't ready to cede any of that control. Plus, she didn't think Ashton wanted her in his daily life as more than a friend. Not really.

He cleared his throat. "What happens if things change?"

"What do you mean?"

"What if you have enough of me?" He grinned. "I plan to do my best so that doesn't happen, but is there an expiration date on us enjoying each other?"

"Depends on how good you are," she teased before going for honesty. "I don't know, Ashton. We'll have to take that one as it comes." Amusement rose. "We've been friends for sixteen years. Maybe we'll be lovers for just as long."

"Maybe." His eyes flashed, heat rising over her skin as his gaze drifted over her. "What do you say we get started on the next sixteen years right now?"

Unexpected. No matter that they'd known each other for years, Sonora still managed to do the unexpected and blow his concentration.

Like now. Not the conversation or all the amazing twists it had taken, but the fact she immediately got to her feet and held out a hand.

The smile she flashed was hot enough to make his knees quiver.

Ashton took her hand and followed, surprised when she stopped by the couch and pulled him down with her.

Another unexpected twist. "No bedroom today?"

"Oh, I'm not saying that at all." Sonora waggled her brows. "I just wanted to start here. I've had a lot of dirty daydreams begin on this couch. It'll be fun to have some real memories to go with them."

On board. Totally on board.

Ashton adjusted position until his arm rested on the backrest, barely brushing her shoulders. His thigh pressed hers, and heat from her torso wrapped around him. The scent of her shampoo, the sound of her breathing—she filled his senses on every level. "I'm very interested in starting."

"Do you have the day off?" Sonora asked.

He barely heard the question. She'd rested her hand on his chest and was teasing her fingers in gentle, barely there circles. "No. Late shift."

"Good enough. No need to rush, then." Sonora's gaze followed her fingers as she undid the top button of his shirt. "The volunteers working the animal rescue will be here between three and five."

"It's only ten," he offered, amazed he could still get the words out. Sonora had leaned in and pressed her lips to his neck. Moist heat, gentle caresses, her in his arms. "You're killing me, woman."

"Hush. I've wanted to do this forever."

She had?

Ashton closed his eyes and fisted his fingers to keep from taking over. Mutual pleasure, she'd said. She'd wanted this? He would allow the torment to continue as long as he could stand.

Sonora moaned, a low, needy sound, and the next moment, she was straddling him. The weight of her ass settling across his thighs set off all sorts of alarms. Ones that said, *Faster, harder, more.*

And when she nipped at his ear, he moved.

Hands on her hips, he lifted her far enough to break the contact between her lips and his neck. The change in position left her mouth free and ready for him to sweep in and take her in a kiss that made it clear he'd been thinking about *this* for a long, long time as well.

Sonora buried her fingers in his hair, the slight sting as she closed her fist and tugged making him feel alive and wild. Needy and bold as he caught the back of her head in his palm and sharpened the angle. Took the kiss deeper, demanded more.

By the time she finally pushed away instead of hauling him forward, they were both gasping for air.

They stared at each other for a moment, and then she smiled. "I look forward to getting to know this side of you."

"You say that now," he warned. "But you don't like it when I'm bossy. And I'm very afraid that's the side that's going to come out."

"In the bedroom?" she teased.

"In the bedroom, on the table, over the back of the damn couch." He'd keep telling her where he planned to take her for days if that dazed expression in her eyes kept getting stronger. "Can you handle that?"

"I can handle you fine, Ashton Stewart. Have been for—"

He took her mouth again, laughing for the first second until her taste overtook him and left all amusement in the dust.

Enjoying the kiss was the first thing on his agenda, and Ashton devoted a good long time to the task. He'd kissed her *that day* so very long ago. But that memory was tangled with sorrow and pain and comfort. Although it had been sexy and hot, it was a priceless treasure that didn't have anything to do with the physical urgency urging them on.

A celebration of life, she'd called it. He remembered her words to this very day. But now? This was a celebration of living. Of experiencing a downright decadent moment of straight-up sexual bliss.

Or at least that was where he was headed.

Sonora had magically undone his buttons, and as she pushed the material back, she growled her displeasure against his mouth. "You're wearing an undershirt," she complained.

He smiled as she shoved his shirt off his shoulders and began tugging at the fabric at his waist. "Almost always. We live in Alberta, and I work with hay and straw. Lots of reasons for a second layer of protection."

Sonora frowned, leaning away. "Off with it."

"Pretty bossy there, darling." He reached over his head and jerked the fabric forward and off in one move. "Your turn."

Sonora removed the long-sleeve sweater that was her top layer. The thin shirt below clung to her curves so sweetly, Ashton had to pause and take a deep breath. He caught her wrists before she could peel the layer away. "I want to eat you up in one big bite. I want to strip you down and have you under me so badly, I can't think. So I don't know why I'm stopping you, but *damn*. Let me touch you like this first."

Was it to prolong the anticipation? To build some memories on top of the innocent moments of admiration from the past years?

All he knew for sure was that she leaned back slightly, breasts pressed to the soft cotton of her shirt, and her smile bewitched him. "Touch me then. But be warned: I get to return the favour."

Ashton rested his palms on her waist. Caressing her body with a controlled focus that said he wasn't going anywhere but that he wasn't about to ravish her.

It was a savouring instead. A small mouthful to tease what would come next. The cotton under his hands was warm from her body. When he slid one hand behind her back, she arched closer and hummed her approval.

The move lifted her breasts toward him like a present. Ashton grinned and accepted the gift, easing a hand forward and filling his palm with soft goodness.

The peak of her nipple teased his flesh as Ashton leaned in and took her lips again. Slower this time. Lightly biting her lower lip, he shared heated air with her while he brushed his thumb back and forth until he needed more.

Her hands roamed over his torso, fingernails scratching lightly. "Let me take my shirt off," she suggested.

"No need." Ashton slid a hand under the fabric and regained his hold, the thin layer of her bra now all that was between them.

"I feel like a kid." Sonora trailed her fingers up his neck then traced his lips slowly, gaze fixed as she played. "As if I'm doing something I'm going to get in trouble for."

"No one's about to walk in on us," Ashton assured her. "But if they did, we're consenting adults. You're not in any trouble."

Or not yet anyway.

"Do you want to use condoms?" he asked. "And if yes, do you have any?"

She laughed. "Does this mean you don't carry them at all times?"

"I usually do, to be honest. Mostly to give to the hands I think are planning unwise moves."

Sonora's amusement grew. "I usually have them around to

be able to give to the girls or their friends considering the same."

Usually. Which meant he'd be getting creative this time. "Next time, I'll be ready."

"Good idea." She pressed her hands to his cheeks and kissed him again. A sweet, hungry motion that made him ready to toss *slow* out the window.

Sonora's phone rang. They both went motionless.

"Ignore it," Ashton suggested, but she had already wiggled off his lap then headed for her purse and hit a couple of buttons on her phone.

"Hi, Sophie." Sonora wrinkled her nose as she glanced back at Ashton. "Sorry, I should have called to tell you I had a change of plans. With the weather turning bad, Ashton brought me home."

Sophie's answer rang out loud over the speaker. "I'm glad you're safe. Malachi is on his way."

Damn.

Sonora eyed her phone with disapproval. "Why is he coming over?"

"The storm, Mom. He's bringing you back here. If it gets as bad as they say it might, I don't want you out there by yourself. You could lose power and heat."

"I have a wood-burning fireplace and candles," Sonora drawled. "Perhaps you, Malachi, and Fern should come ride out the storm with me."

"I should've thought of that sooner. Anyway, Malachi will be there in the next ten minutes. Bring the recipe for your chocolate brownies. Fern was asking for some." Sophie hung up

Sonora turned toward Ashton with a look of resignation. "They mean well."

"Not a problem. I get it." He stood and paced toward her.

"Sophie is right. Better for me to be at the ranch as well, just in case. We'll start our new adventure when the time is right."

"Gives us both time to buy condoms," Sonora teased.

Ashton pulled her against him and kissed her one more time. Because he could. Because he wanted to. "Stay safe. I'll talk to you soon."

He made it away from her house before Sonora's son-in-law arrived, the secret of the change between them like a living coal hidden in his chest.

8

———

One good thing came from having spent the night at her daughter's. Sonora eyed the dozen baskets of freshly baked treats currently filling the trunk of Sophie's car with great satisfaction.

"At least our time sitting out 'the storm of the decade' didn't go to waste," Sonora teased.

Sophie stuck out her tongue. "There was still more than two feet of snow overnight. I'm glad it wasn't as terrible as they said it would be. Bad enough there was a big accident on the highway."

"Well, one of the baskets can go to the fire hall," Sonora offered. "I'm sure the team that had the call-out during the storm will appreciate it."

It wasn't the sex-fest pastime Sonora had been hoping for, but she could hardly complain about enjoying the evening with her family. Baking goodies with her youngest granddaughter had given her and Fern time to catch up.

Family had always, and *would* always, come first with Sonora.

Now, as they prepared to deliver the goodies all over town,

Sonora appreciated the snow tires and four-wheel drive on Sophie's vehicle, especially after heading up some of the steeper drives in the community.

The rough weather had fooled them all by being intense but brief, and while there were huge piles of snow everywhere, the sun shone with an almost violent intensity. The temperature hovered just above freezing instead of the chilling cold they'd had a few days ago.

Sophie glanced at her as they approached Lone Pine ranch. "It must feel strange to be coming up here and not have Connie there to greet you."

"It's never easy to lose a friend," Sonora agreed. Connie had been one of the special joys of moving to Heart Falls. She'd passed away from cancer three Christmases ago, and the ache was still there. "I'm glad Patrick has family living with him now. It would've been exceptionally lonely if he didn't have Brad and Hanna and Crissy."

"A little bit lonely like your house gets?" Sophie asked quietly.

Maybe, but Sonora wasn't ready to give up her freedom yet. "It does get lonely at times, but it's lonely in a way I like. Would I enjoy having another person there? Some of the time. But I still feel as if I'm learning how to be the best me I can, and that's easier when I'm not listening to the voices of others."

Except, of course, the voice of her husband as he, or it, or whatever her psyche should be called, taunted her with undeniable truths.

Damn ghost.

"As long as you're still sure." Sophie pulled to a stop outside the cabin. She laid her hand on Sonora's arm. "You don't have to know the exact next steps to say you're ready for a change. I promise we won't pick you up and move you the instant you say something. If you're worried about that."

"It's kind of scary how smart you are," Sonora said.

Sophie winked. "I learned from the best."

The front door opened before they even hit the doorbell. Hanna Ford stood there with a welcoming smile, gesturing them forward. "Come in before we lose all the heat."

Crissy raced up to the door, the eleven-year-old grinning widely. "Grandpa is in the living room. You want to see him?"

"Grandpa is right here, you rascal." Patrick leaned on his cane and wiggled the fingers of one hand in greeting. "Just because you can run faster than me doesn't mean I can't get where I want to go."

"If they visit with you in the living room, I can bring you tea and cookies," Crissy offered.

"Which means she can dip into the cookie jar again and undoubtably enjoy another fistful herself," Hanna said quietly as she conspiratorially leaned her head toward Sonora.

"We'd love some tea," Sophie told Crissy seriously. "And we brought some treats. Maybe you can put them in the living room so your grandpa can have first pick?"

Patrick clapped his hands together. "Christmas baking. One of my favorite things."

Sophie took off her coat then escorted Patrick to the living room. Crissy took off to the kitchen, but Hanna stayed behind to help Sonora hang up her things.

Or at least that seemed to be the excuse she gave.

Sonora eyed the younger woman carefully. There was a glow about her, and when Hanna smoothed her bright red Christmas shirt over her stomach, a soft smile on her lips, Sonora's suspicions grew.

Hanna glanced up then blushed. "Oops?"

"I'm not going to ask," Sonora informed her. "If you have something to tell me, that's a thing you need to say outright."

Hanna glanced behind them then stepped closer. "Crissy doesn't know yet, but yes. I'm expecting in June."

Sonora hugged the young woman tightly. Next steps were

always big and important no matter how ordinary they were. "Connie would have been very pleased with the family you're building here with Brad."

Hanna's eyes were bright when she stepped back. "Brad is thrilled, and so is Patrick."

"Rightly so." Sonora pressed her finger to her lips. "Now let's go see if Crissy left any of the baking for Patrick."

Hanna wrapped an arm around Sonora and led her to the living room, laughter dancing around them.

An hour later, Sonora and Patrick were finishing their game of crib while Hanna and Crissy took Sophie to the barn for a quick kitten cuddle.

"You're up to mischief," Patrick announced across the game board.

Sonora blinked, glancing at her hand. "I'm not cheating."

Patrick folded his arms over his chest, shaking his head from side to side. "Not talking about cards." He leaned toward her, gaze narrowing. "Your expression. I've seen that one before. It means you're up to no good."

"Really?" Sonora put as much shock and disbelief into her tone as possible.

He eyed her, amusement curling his lips. "You wore that same expression back when you and Connie organized the first bachelor auction."

Sonora smiled sweetly at him. "And a very successful annual fundraiser it's become."

"And another time, you somehow got Connie tangled up in a bet that concluded with the local café being named after her." Patrick shook his head. "Okay, that one is amusing. I hear Stephanie and Jason have to explain all the time that, yes, Connie was a real person, but no, she's not some relative of theirs or a former owner."

"Just someone who was very good at trivia," Sonora reminded Patrick. "It was Stephanie's fault, really. Everyone else in town knew better than to go head to head against Connie with Trivial Pursuit on the line."

Patrick picked up his cards again and adjusted them. He slid one to the opposite side then back, killing time. "I'm just saying I've known you for a very long time, Sonora. I want good things for you, which means if you are plotting trouble, I hope it's the best kind of mischief. Remember, if you ever need anything, I might not be Connie, but I'm still your friend."

Sonora laid a hand over his. "I know. And I'm thankful. Whatever mischief I plan, I promise I'll be careful and enjoy myself at the same time."

And then she really hoped Ashton wouldn't stop by anytime in the next while because Patrick was a good enough friend to *both* of them to be able to put two and two together and come up with shenanigans.

As her granddaughters had taken to calling mischief.

Sonora gave Patrick a big hug when it was time to go, accepted a hug and a kiss from Crissy, and gave Hanna one final squeeze.

Sophie offered a happy sigh as they made their way down the narrow road back to Heart Falls. "I'm so happy for them. They've had some tough moments over the past years, but they've come out together and growing."

"Just like our family," Sonora offered. She smiled at her daughter. "Ivy and Walker are a delight. Rose and Tansy are blooming with what they're doing. I know the success of their shop has been possible because you and Malachi helped guide them."

"You offered money to help them open the doors in the first place," Sophie returned softly. "Family cares for each other, however we need it."

"What does Fern need?" Sonora asked, genuinely interested. The night they'd spent baking together had been sweet, but Fern didn't spill secrets easily. Whatever was on her youngest granddaughter's mind had stayed tightly hidden. "She seems happily involved in many things, but I don't assume that she's not searching as well."

"I think she's good for now, but you're right. We'll keep watching." Sophie pointed the car toward the fire hall. "One more drop-off, and then I'll take you home."

Sonora's house was cold when she walked in, but it didn't take much to get the fireplace burning brightly. She deliberately made herself a cup of tea and sat on the couch to consider her options.

They might've both agreed to the relationship change that would broaden the scope of what they had, but first and foremost, she and Ashton were friends. Simply contacting him for a booty call was not how she planned to roll.

They had said it yesterday. Sixteen years of being friends. What would sixteen years of being lovers look like? And how would they combine the two?

She considered what she knew of his routine before she pulled out her phone and sent a text.

Sonora: *I assume you're sleeping right now after your night shift. Come over for supper tomorrow night if that works. You can bring dessert.*

She was about to put the phone away when she realized her mistake. Texting Ashton was a long shot. The chance he'd open his messages was slim.

She wasn't about to also leave him a phone message or send an email, because one message asking him to come for a meal, with its implied *sex me after*, was enough. Two contacts struck her as desperate, and three would be beyond pathetic. That many attempts to reach him would send up signals that she planned to be needy and demanding, and that was not the idea behind this change of circumstances.

Sonora sighed. It would have been nice if they could have enjoyed one more uninterrupted hour yesterday.

When Ashton didn't text or call or message her on Sunday or the following morning, she simply shook her head in amusement and took it in stride.

But by late Monday afternoon, she really wanted to know when they could see each other next.

She was about to call him when a gust of wind nearly took off the roof. Sonora rushed to the window and watched the snow begin to fall so hard and fast, she couldn't see her driveway.

So much for having gotten away from the predicted nasty weather. The storm of the decade had finally arrived.

"The heat is out in the cookhouse." Luke Stone shoved the door shut behind him and knocked the snow off his shoulders as he marched toward where Ashton was holding an emergency meeting with the hands.

"You got things working the last time this happened." Caleb tilted his head toward Ashton. "Think you can do it again? Because the chance of getting an electrician out right now is nil."

"Send someone with me so I have an extra set of hands, and I'll try." Ashton gestured to the men gathered to his right. "There are still animals out in the north field. We need to get them into the shelters and out of the wind. Stay with your partner, and move the animals toward the ravine if you can. They'll be more willing to walk away from the wind than toward it," he reminded them.

This wasn't how Ashton had planned the day to go. He'd made a list of all the work tasks he had to do and tossed in a couple of things for friends, but getting together with Sonora had been the ultimate goal.

Part of the morning had been spent looking up information about the star Brooke had asked about. The sky had been a gorgeous bright blue when he'd finally tracked down Mack to let him know where to go check.

Damn. He hoped Mack hadn't done something foolish like head out after it. Ashton pulled out his phone to send a warning message and discovered Sonora's days-old invitation to dinner.

Another thing Ashton wouldn't be doing until the weather settled.

Caleb joined the hands, making sure they had the equipment they needed to stay safe.

Luke walked with Ashton as they cut through the barns and headed to the cookhouse. "And here I'd thought we'd managed to avoid the storm."

"I'd give you guff about counting your chickens before they hatched, but I had hoped the same thing," Ashton admitted. He loved his job, loved working at Silver Stone. But he had hoped to be heading to Sonora's right about now.

Instead he and Luke worked for an hour before successfully finding the failed power circuit. Once the power was back on at the cookhouse, another task that absolutely needed doing beckoned. And another.

Luke stayed with him, though, and Ashton was grateful for the company. They hit the coffee pot and topped up mugs with the dark, steamy java, pausing to shoot the breeze.

Ashton eyed the younger man. "Tell me what you and Kelli have planned for the new year."

"Not much out of the ordinary," Luke admitted, but he flashed a grin. "Just being together is still such a kick I have to admit that *ordinary* never feels it."

"You two belong together," Ashton said simply.

"Now that you no longer want to rip off my ears?" Luke teased.

Ashton raised a brow. "It wasn't your ears that were in danger."

Luke laughed, but he winced slightly. "Point taken."

Kelli James, now Kelli Stone, had been the lone female hand at Silver Stone for many years, and Ashton had more than felt the need to watch out for her. She and Luke hitting it off over the past year had been a good thing.

Damn his brother for constantly suggesting Ashton had no children. He had so many people he was invested in seeing grow up right, it was outrageous.

Monday evening vanished in a rash of chores and dealing with the storm. Ashton barely had time to breathe, but he did finally eke out a moment to respond to Sonora's invitation.

Ashton: *Sorry. I got this late, and as you can tell, the weather gods are currently against us. Rain check?*

It was Tuesday morning before he had another chance to check for her response.

Sonora: *Technology is wasted on you. It really is.*

Sonora: *Of course, rain check. I hope all is well at Silver Stone. I'm trapped at the house, but I have plenty of firewood and no problems with electricity. The animals in the shelter are all fine. I don't have many right now, anyway.*

Sonora: *We'll worry about seeing each other after the holidays. Merry Christmas, Ashton.*

That was it. The extent of her concern.

It was...odd, yet right. They'd never lived in each other's

pockets before, and while he wanted to dive into the next stage with her—

There was no rush.

Or at least that's what he tried to tell himself when he woke up on Christmas Day with a hard-on and dirty dreams still running through his brain.

Traditions were wonderful things, yet at that moment, Ashton wished he could throw the entire holiday season into the trash barrel.

Usually, coming over to the main ranch house at the Stones' was like enjoying a warm hug. Since their parents had passed, Caleb and his siblings had done their best to build new memories. There had been a few years when scrambling to get everything done had caused a bit of a panic until Ashton suggested they not try to do things up early.

Which meant Christmas Eve after the young ones were in bed was when the tree magically went up. In the early years, it had only been Dustin who woke up to the surprise of presents and tinsel and cinnamon on the air. The first years after his friends died, Ashton had been there both the night before, helping trim the tree, and first thing in the morning.

Some of the traditions had changed. Now that Caleb and Tamara were happily settled in the home and the other older boys were married and living close by, Ashton's task was reduced to coming for Christmas dinner at noon and bringing his fiddle to play afterward.

What he wanted to do was head over to Sonora's house, but with the snow over the past forty-eight hours finally at an end, no way could he simply take off. Besides, she'd be with the Fields family. Sonora, her unmarried granddaughters, and Ivy and Walker had gathered with Sophie and Malachi that morning, and it was right.

She belonged there. He belonged here.

Ashton enjoyed the meal and the laughter. He played a set

of songs as the children danced and happiness filled the house. Walker arrived with Ivy, soon tucking her into a quiet corner to be part of the gathering in their own way, and the family seemed to pull together even tighter right before Ashton's eyes.

The thought came hard and fast. *What my brother Steve has with Lynn is nothing like what the Stones have created.*

Ashton sat silently for a moment, wondering why that truth had registered out of nowhere. It was true—absolutely.

It wasn't that marriage was a terrible thing. Caleb and Tamara, and Walter and Deb before them, were proving that. The moment between, where Caleb's first marriage had failed, was also true, but the positive building blocks his friends had begun stood as a base for something wonderful. Walker and Ivy. Luke and Kelli.

"You seem distracted." Caleb laid a hand on Ashton's shoulder. "Worried about fallout from the storm?"

Ashton glanced at the man, his brain scrambling to catch up. It was as good an excuse as any, but then again, he didn't want Caleb to think the worst. "Everyone did what needed to be done. Just got a lot on my mind."

Caleb squeezed gently then sat beside him. "Changes happen slowly, it seems. The weather, the animals." He glanced around the room at his brothers with their wives and his children happily interacting with their uncles and aunts. "Lots of good changes."

"I agree."

Caleb didn't look at him, but his next words were pointed. "You take the changes you need too. You're a rock-solid part of this family, but that doesn't mean you have to be a rock."

Ashton paused. The words were enough to make him sit back and consider the man before him. He truly looked at Caleb and saw someone new.

No longer was Caleb the young man he'd been all those

years ago, overwhelmed as the weight of responsibility dropped on him out of time and circumstance.

He was older of course, but it was his sense of purpose and self that made Caleb immovable in all the right ways. He had a wife who supported him and nudged him when he veered off the path. He had children to give him a purpose to aim forward and family members strong enough to lift him up.

Caleb didn't need Ashton the same way he had before. The knowledge was good yet soul-shaking.

He'd need more time to truly let the change sink in, but for now Ashton dipped his chin and listened to the heartfelt message behind the words. "I like being a part of the family. And I don't feel hard done by or trapped," he insisted honestly.

"I'm glad," Caleb said, his gaze drifting over his family once again. "I want you to always feel you have a place at Silver Stone. And this isn't a hint at all, but when you want to shake things up, when you don't want to be the one crawling around power poles in the middle of a storm, let me know. You could consider bringing on an apprentice for a few years if you'd like. Make the transition smoother."

"Make them crawl up the power pole?"

Caleb grinned. "Maybe. When you're ready, we'll talk about what comes next. Deal?"

"I'm not at that point yet, but deal," Ashton agreed.

The conversation broke as Tamara marched over and handed off eight-month-old Tyler to Ashton. "You owe me a dance," she said to Caleb, tugging him to his feet.

To the children's delight, Caleb whirled Tamara into the open floor off the kitchen. Luke turned up the radio then caught Kelli in his embrace. Walker held open his arms, and Ivy joined him, and then they were all dancing, moving together with joy and happiness and a sense of rightness that made Ashton's heart warm.

Good people. Good, solid people he was so fortunate to have in his world.

He slipped away a little later, that warm glow sticking with him as he stepped into the wintery night. His dog, Beauty, joined him briefly for a quick pet before racing back to the warmth of the barn to join the other ranch dogs.

Ashton was halfway back across the yard when he noticed another warm glow, this one radiating from his bunkhouse windows. It was pretty, but at the same time, he glanced around to see if any of the hands were in view.

He'd harped on conserving energy and turning off lights far too often to get away without a razzing. The damned part was he was sure he'd shut them off. Obviously, he hadn't.

He grumbled as he walked through the door and then jerked to a stop.

It wasn't an overhead light he'd left on. Sonora was there, curled up on his couch. A small plug-in Christmas tree with bright yellow lights at the end of each branch glowed against the nearest wall.

"You're here." Asinine thing to say, but it was all he had.

"I am," she offered, putting down her book and rising to her feet. She paced toward him, smile in place. "I hope you don't mind me inviting myself over. But I had a gift I want to give you, and it is still Christmas Day."

That's when he noticed what she was wearing. The silvery robe that hung barely past her knees was held closed by a bright red ribbon tied around her waist.

Ashton lifted his gaze to meet hers. "Merry Christmas to me."

9

———

It had seemed necessary. After their plans had been messed up by family and Mother Nature, taking charge of the situation was the only viable option.

And while it had involved some juggling, Sonora was pleased with the results.

Especially with the way Ashton was looking at her.

"Not that I want to get into tons of details, but how did you get here?" Ashton asked as he rid himself of his boots and coat then stepped toward her.

"Rose and Tansy picked me up en route to the Fields family gathering this morning. Sophie lent me her truck to get home. Which means I've got a vehicle with great traction, so you don't have to worry about me when I leave. And in case you're wondering, I parked in the hands' parking lot then walked through the barns. No one saw me."

"Which is probably a detail I should spend a lot more mental energy on, but I'm kind of distracted at the moment." He teased his fingers down the front of her robe, and her nipples beaded instantly. "In spite of the risk of you saying no, I'll ask again. Are you sure you want this? Now? Tonight?"

"I didn't think there was an expiration date on the offer or anything. I just want to be with you," Sonora said plainly.

Those talented fingers drifted upward, pausing as he discovered one rigid peak. He curled a finger and stroked his knuckle over the tip, and her entire body lit with anticipation.

"I'm glad." Ashton slid his other hand around her back and tugged their torsos together. "Very glad."

She glanced up, he leaned down, and their mouths made contact once again. This time was less of a shock but nowhere near familiar. Still absolutely nerve-tingling and body-aching, the anticipation of pleasure sent small pulses radiating from her core.

"Thank you for my Christmas tree," he whispered against her lips.

She slid her hands along the waistline of his jeans until she caught a big enough fistful of the fabric to begin to undress him. "Check out the decorations a little closer."

He kept her against his torso as he twisted his head to the side. A sharp burst of laughter escaped as he peeked at the shiny packages hanging from the branches. "Did you make those?"

"I did. Saw them on Pinterest," she drawled.

Ashton leaned to the side and nabbed one of the snowmen from the tree. Three silver condom packages were glued together strategically, with googly eyes and coloured pieces of construction paper to create the nose, mouth, and buttons.

"I don't know what kind of twisted significance snowmen and sex are supposed to have, but thank you for the supply."

"No hidden messages, I promise." Sonora eased her hands under his shirt. Hot male skin met her palms, and she sighed happily. "Please get naked."

His answer was to reach for the belt of her robe and slowly undo it. He separated the fabric, and his breathing kicked up a notch. She hadn't built up the nerve to go completely naked under the robe. Her prettiest bra-and-pantie set gave her the courage to keep her chin lifted as his gaze swept over her.

Ashton's fingers went first to her tattoo, the barely there touch teasing as he stroked over the lines that had been added in the years since their last time together. "Sonora. It's beautiful." His eyes met hers. "You're beautiful."

He slid his palms around her body and down her back until he cupped her ass. When he pulled her against him, the sides of the robe fell open and left her naked skin to brush against his cotton shirt and the rougher fabric of his jeans.

His lips on hers felt right. Made her ache inside as he coaxed her tongue to tangle with his. He planted a line of kisses along her jaw all the way to the spot under her ear, sending a shiver rolling over her from top to bottom.

As they kissed, she touched him everywhere. Hands over his arms, fingertips stroking his biceps and triceps with deep appreciation. Roaming over the muscles of his back and down the line of his spine, Sonora savoured the contact until he was the one groaning.

Still kissing, Ashton guided them into his bedroom. She felt zero guilt at having already been in the room, making sure it was prepared for this moment. She hadn't been worried about finding a mess, not with how disciplined he was. But as the backs of her knees hit the mattress, she knew the quilt was already pulled back, and nothing would get in the way of them continuing the journey they'd begun.

A low chuckle escaped him as he half scooped her up and placed her on the mattress before crawling beside her. "I seem to have had a visit from Goldilocks. Was the bed too firm or too soft?"

Sonora opened her legs and let his hips settle between her thighs. "Just right. Especially now."

They kissed again, but even as their tongues sparred, she lifted her hips to rock against the hard length that was his fully engaged cock. Her senses spun, and when she sucked his tongue into her mouth, his hips jerked automatically.

Ashton gasped for air as he pulled back. "You keep doing that, and I'm not going to last," he warned.

"There's no quota involved either." The mock glare she offered him didn't faze him at all. "You really aren't very good at taking orders, are you? You're supposed to be naked."

"Not until I take you over at least once." His voice was so deep and husky, it brushed her skin like a physical caress.

He slid a hand over her belly until he cupped her mound.

A soft curse escaped as he dipped thick fingers between her folds. He licked his lips. "You're wet."

"I've been thinking about you and what we could get up to for a couple of hours," she pointed out. "That's enough time to get anyone's motor stoked."

"Good to know." He eased his fingers a little deeper before pulling them back, a gentle caress over her clit that felt amazing.

"Do that again," she demanded

His grin was downright evil. "Something else I need to do first."

He kept his hand cradled over her mound possessively as he lowered his head to her breast before closing his lips around a nipple.

Sensation followed sensation. The sensitive peaks reacted to the heat of his mouth and the languid rasp of his tongue. That alone would've been enough to bring her pleasure after years of denied touch.

But combined with the way he teased with his fingers, the smallest of movements with the most intimate caress—

Sonora closed her eyes, wrapped her hands around his shoulders, and let him take control.

❧

ASHTON COULDN'T REMEMBER the last time he'd been so turned on so quickly. It wasn't only that the woman was beautiful, but she was…

Sonora. Not just curves and dips but attitude and sass and power.

Staying slow took every bit of control he had. The noises from her lips, the little gasps and moans, heated him up and sent need sizzling along his nerves. Sent a pulse that wrapped around his cock and balls and made his brain cells short-circuit.

He slipped a finger farther into her sheath, and she sucked in air. Muscles clutched tight as he stroked inside while brushing her clit with his thumb.

"Yes, do that again." Sonora swore, opening her legs farther to ease his movements. Ashton smiled and returned his head to her breast, suckling right through the fabric. Fucking two fingers into her, he nuzzled aside her bra and lapped hard at her nipple until her pussy tightened around his hand, her climax beginning.

He stripped off his boxers, pulled her to the edge of the bed, and after ridding her of her panties, dropped his mouth over her pulsing core.

She cried out with delight and buried her fingers in his hair. Sonora went wild, arching harder into his mouth, chanting his name, still coming hard around his fingers, and he was on the edge of joining her.

He fought for control and just barely won. He danced his tongue over her clit, stroked her labia, and plunged his fingers into her core again and again until another wave broke. Only then did he move.

It took a moment to pull a condom from his side table and cover himself, and then he was up and over her body. The tip of his cock centered against her sex, he paused to examine her face. He saw nothing there but pleasure and anticipation.

Ashton stared into her eyes as he pressed into her heat in one smooth motion.

Her soft coo of pleasure was exactly what he needed to hear. That Sonora lifted her feet and wrapped her legs around him to seal them closer made it even better. Ashton trembled on the edge of control.

Sonora dug her fingernails into his back and scratched slowly. "More," she demanded.

Fuck. Ashton thrust.

No longer slow, each thrust was harder and faster than the one before, driving her back into the bed, driving him as deep into her welcoming folds as possible. Sonora's grin widened, and he felt like laughing. Being together was hot and heavenly with no expectations beyond this moment, this feeling.

A loud *bang* intruded.

From the other side of the wall, a constant thumping sound echoed into his room, and Sonora laughed out loud. "Really?"

Jeez. Ashton shook his head. "New hand. Moved in just a few days ago."

Her smile widened even as she rocked toward him, encouraging him to keep moving. "He has no idea your rooms back his, does he?"

Ashton would have laughed as well, but everything in him was focused on the pleasure rising between them. His bed rocked silently with their exertions—thank God *he* was smart enough to not plant the bed frame right against the wall, or they'd be declaring what was going on in the foreman's rooms to the entire ranch as well.

Sonora grabbed his ass and pulled him harder into her on the next thrust, lifting her hips to meet him. She placed her heels to his butt, noises of pleasure rising louder and quicker around them.

"Yes, so close." Sonora licked his chest and squirmed.

Normally he'd slow down, reach between them, and help

her climax, but he was beyond the point of no return. His balls drew up so tight against his body, they nearly disappeared, and he was barely aware of her hand sneaking between them to rub her clit.

The next moment, he exploded, his whole body jerking with reaction as the feel of her touching him, squeezing him, overwhelmed his senses. Under him, she shook with her climax, and then they were both boneless, laughing together on the bed as constant thumping continued from the room behind his.

"Do you think they'll be long?" Sonora asked, her face full of mischief.

He traced a hand over her body and watched a shiver run ahead of his caress. "He's going to be very embarrassed when he finds out."

She laughed again. Amusement turned to a hum as he stroked a line of her tattoo. "I enjoyed that, Ashton. Very much."

"Me too."

The bangs sped up, and they both smothered snickers. Sonora sighed contentedly then eyed the wall. "He's enthusiastic. Got to give him points for that."

"Instead of listening to someone else, I'd prefer to make you moan my name again."

Her face lit up, and Ashton's body responded instantly. Dammit, he was like a teenager around her.

"Shower?" he suggested. "The banging might be done by the time we get out."

Sonora stood without a blush and headed for the bathroom. She pivoted in the doorway, and he got a long look at her body, the soft silvery strands of her hair sliding over her shoulders. "I have until midnight," she announced.

"You have a pumpkin to catch?" He joined her at the door and turned on the taps.

They stepped into the shower. Ashton hummed with approval as she picked up the soap and rubbed to create a handful of lather. "No, but I have things I need to do tomorrow, and I need a full night's sleep. It's probably best that my truck is gone before the morning." She rubbed a soapy hand over his chest and leaned in for a kiss. "Time enough for another round if you're up for it."

Ashton kissed her gently before he pulled away. She was too good to be true. "No expiration date, no quota," he reminded her.

Sonora shrugged. "It's been a long time, and I enjoyed myself." Her hands moved lower on his body, and he shivered as she took firm possession of his cock.

"Until midnight, hmm?" He checked the time on the bedside digital clock just visible through the open bathroom door.

She seemed fascinated by what she was doing with her hands. "Yup."

He was going to die a happy man. He closed his eyes and let her play. They had hours ahead of them. Spending his strength on the woman was going to be very entertaining and satisfying.

THAT FIRST NIGHT led to another a few days later and then to more fun than Ashton had dreamed possible. In and out of bed, Sonora became his very willing partner in debauchery.

No, that was wrong. Things got dirty between them all right, but there was always a thread of such joy and decency in the sex that Ashton figured he'd hit the jackpot.

He found ways to sneak over to her place. She turned up at the ranch at the strangest times and places, willing to jump him in the tack room or in the hayloft.

One fine spring day, he opened the door of a tractor and

found her waiting inside. The logistics of that encounter would have stymied a less resourceful man.

Ashton was resourceful.

Today's midsummer fishing trip had become more about teasing each other to wildly pleasurable releases than tracking down the elusive rainbow trout.

They'd just finished a rather vigorous interlude, and Sonora was still making the most delicious noises as she lay beside him on the heavy picnic blanket he'd laid on the riverbank.

Ashton rolled to his side and chuckled. "You deflating over there?"

She twisted her head toward him, the rosy flush of her cheeks making her eyes shine even brighter. "What's that?"

"You're sighing and exhaling so hard, I figure you've sprung a leak."

Her laughter floated over the sunshine-dappled water sparkling at their feet. "Maybe you pumped me full of air. That was rather athletic, Ashton."

"I've been eating my Wheaties." He leaned in close and kissed her. Soft and tender. Damn if this being together on a regular basis thing wasn't the icing on the cake that he'd been missing his entire life. "Thanks for joining me."

"I like fishing," she said with an absolutely straight face.

"Ha. So do I." He let his gaze slide over her in admiration. Naked or dressed, Sonora clicked all his buttons. He wasn't shocked at the lengths he'd go to wrangle some alone time with her. "But the boys are going to tease me about how shitty my luck has gotten when I come home yet again with no fish."

"Yeah, too bad you're not getting lucky." Her lips curled into a full grin as she sat upright and reached for her clothes.

He put a hand on her shoulder to stop her from covering up. "Cold?"

She shook her head. "Not really."

Ashton crowded her back on the blanket, covering her with his body. "I want to look at your tattoo again."

"Obsessed."

"Maybe." Although he didn't think it was the tattoo as much as the canvas beneath it. But Sonora stretched out, rolling slightly, humming happily as he drifted his fingers down her side to trace the pattern again.

He'd done this dozens of times since they'd officially become lovers, but each time he spotted something new. "Your tattoo artist is amazing."

"She is. Some of the design, Fern created," she reminded him.

"So talented." He stroked the tiny leaves unfurling along her hip bone. "That they're not just lines but lines of text makes it even more meaningful." Ashton pressed a kiss to the tiny rock pile created by Walter and Deb's names. "The stones."

"A cornerstone," she said.

Ashton pulled back and looked at the bigger image more closely. Well, damn if she wasn't right. "I didn't see that before."

Sonora stroked her fingers through his hair. "They did one of the hardest things. They created a safe place for their children to grow even after they were gone. And you were part of that," she reminded him.

He slid beside her and pulled her into his arms. "I guess I was. Still am." He pressed his lips to her temple and let the heat of her body warm him through. "I guess I always will be."

They were in the middle of pulling on clothes when a bell went off, and Sonora whooped. She shoved her feet into her boots and hurried a short distance down the river.

He followed, laughing as he spotted the fishing line and bobber merrily dancing.

She landed a nice-sized trout then presented it to him with a grin. "Here. It's yours. Take it and show it off to the boys so your reputation stays intact for another day."

Damn beautiful. Damn smart. Ashton accepted the fish as if it were a gold medal.

Life continued, full and entertaining. Work at Silver Stone remained steady and full. Ashton was asked to help at the local fire hall, and spending time with the other coordinators filled the need in him to give to the community beyond the ranch.

He and Sonora continued to meet in secret. Sometimes weekly, sometimes longer between touching base, but every time they got together, their connection stayed as brilliantly happy and sizzling hot. Sonora seemed content. And Ashton?

Ashton took each day and savoured it to the fullest.

10

December, one year ago

"Rummy."

Ashton cursed as a grinning Gary Silver dramatically laid his cards on the table. "How the hell do you do that? We've only had one round of play, and you're out again?"

Gary shrugged as he gathered the cards together and began to shuffle them. "Clean living combined with my extreme intelligence."

The third man at the table, James, gave Gary a dirty look. "More like horseshoes up your ass."

"Language," Ashton said automatically just because he knew it would make his friends laugh.

The music pumping around them was a nice background to the companionship at the table. Rough Cut pub had a limited menu, but the plain fare of burgers and a bag of chips was enough for their gathering, especially when paired with a pint.

As far as that went, the dining options in town were limited, unless they wanted to hit the local diner yet again or pay for a fancy meal at the couple of high-end places nearby.

Burger and beer? Rough Cut all the way.

The dance floor was busy on this Friday night, but the table Ashton and his friends had commandeered along the side was relatively quiet. The owner of the establishment and a fellow volunteer at the fire hall, Ryan Zhao, paced up and reloaded their glasses. "You gentlemen need to watch yourself. Any wilder behaviour, and I'll cut you off."

"Speaking of wild behaviour." Ashton looked the man over then glanced at the bar. "Was nice to meet your friend Madison the other night at the fire hall."

Ryan's face lit up. "Best friend from forever ago. She's sticking around for the rest of the month."

"Glad to hear it." Ashton glanced over at the woman chatting easily with Ryan's assistant as the two moved in a steady rhythm behind the bar, pulling drinks. The dark bruises under Madison's eyes gave up all kinds of warning signals, so it had been good to discover the damage was from a car mishap and not something a human inflicted.

Ryan stepped away, and Gary leaned in to speak so he didn't have to shout. "Brooke hauled in Madison's car for us to fix. It wasn't in too rough a shape, but damn, those airbags did a number on the girl."

"The little firecracker behind the bar?" James asked before turning back to the cards. "If she's hanging out with Ryan, she's in good hands."

Ashton agreed. He'd gotten to know Ryan over the past months at the fire hall. The man was steady and tireless.

James shuffled the cards and held them up enquiringly. "Another round?"

"In a minute. Be right back." Ashton gave his friends a nod

then headed toward the restroom. En route, he spotted a couple of Silver Stone's less reputable hands.

It was instinct to weave his way through the growing crowd to within hearing distance, especially after he noticed the pointed glances aimed in Madison's direction while she worked behind the bar.

"I'd tap that." Jim tilted his chin toward her, an assessing leer in his eyes.

"Me too. Want to see who's the better man?" Michael suggested. "Bet I can get into her pants before midnight."

"Ha. You're in and out so fast, they don't even notice."

"Oh, they notice," Mike bragged. "Walk bowlegged for days afterward."

For fuck's sake. Was this what kids these days felt was worth bragging about? Ashton stepped between them and the bar, cutting off their view of Madison. "If the woman is interested in either of you, I assume she'll let you know. But all things considered, you should probably aim your attentions elsewhere."

The men pulled back instinctively. "Hey, Ashton. Didn't see you there," Jim said.

"I figured," Ashton drawled.

Mike and Jim exchanged glances. "We were only kidding around. You know how it is."

"And I'm only reminding you to watch your manners. Got no problem with you enjoying time with the ladies as long as they're enjoying themselves as well." Ashton gave Jim a pointed glare. "Aren't you seeing someone regularly?"

The man had the grace to look uncomfortable before pulling his bluster back into place. "It's more of an on-again, off-again thing."

"Really?" The disbelief in his tone was deadly. "Okay. You gentlemen have a good evening, and I'll see you on shift tomorrow." Ashton gave them his firmest stare. "Don't be late."

He didn't know what made them so fucked up, a lack of training or lack of give-a-shit, but it was sad to see. Ashton hit the john then paused outside the door. He settled on the bench in the shadows to pull off his boot and deal with the rock that had plagued him all night.

"Bad timing on Ashton overhearing us," Mike complained as he shouldered toward the restroom.

"Fucker needs to get laid. Maybe then he'd be in a better mood once in a while."

"Nah, it's not the lack of sex. I think he's actually that much of a bastard. He and that Fallen woman are knocking boots on a regular basis."

"Get out. That's just a rumour," Jim insisted.

"Don't think so. I caught him mooning after her one day when she stopped by to drop off something for her son-in-law." Mike chuckled. "She's old, but she's still a knockout. Must be freaky in bed because the bastard seems to always have a smile on his face after she leaves. Check it out sometime."

Jim pushed through the restroom door, his voice fading as it closed behind him. "Him getting it on the regular? That would be unfair."

"You really didn't know? We could make some money on this," Mike suggested. "Just saying."

Ashton waited until he was certain the men wouldn't spot him then hightailed it back to the table with his friends, cursing himself yet thankful he'd overheard the conversation.

It wasn't just the grossness of being discussed like that. They always said eavesdroppers heard bad things about themselves.

Bad things being said about Sonora didn't sit nearly so well.

∼

Ashton pondered all night, but by the next morning, he figured he might have a solution. Made him feel an absolute fool, but it needed to be done. Anything to get wagging tongues and eyes off Sonora.

Thankfully, he had a good reason to stop by the animal shelter. Ashton hoisted the extra bag of dog food Silver Stone had ordered as a donation and made his way into the barn outside Sonora's house.

The place had gone through a number of changes over the years since she'd moved in. While she'd never had more than a few animals herself, she'd done a good job of making the place as comfortable for them as possible.

He'd also had a hand in the early years, creating systems to allow her to be as independent as possible when it came to saddling her horse and the rest of it. Equipment was heavy, and while she was in shape, there was no reason she needed to store saddles or feed bins way up high like they did at Silver Stone.

"Hey, Ashton." Charity Gruzing paced past him, a couple of kittens squirming in her arms. The woman was also a volunteer on the fire team. "Looking for a place to put that?"

"Figured the storage room. Get the door for me?" he asked.

"No problem." She juggled kittens for a bit then managed to help him out. "I'll tell Sonora you're here."

"She in the barn?"

"She was cleaning a stall. That way." One of the kittens crawled out of Charity's grasp, and the young woman scrambled after it. "Drat."

Ashton laughed. "Have fun."

Then he tracked Sonora down.

She was cleaning an old stall. She raked slowly, and the scratch of the rake prongs pulling bedding into order was a soft brush on his eardrums.

"Hey."

"Hey." Sonora smiled up at him. "Want me to put you to work?"

"Not hardly. I only have a minute, but I need to talk to you."

She leaned the rake on the wall. "Shoot."

Sharing what he'd overheard at the bar made him feel like crap. Thankfully, Sonora didn't seem as upset about it as he was.

Still, this needed to be fixed, and soon. "I think we should have a fight."

She rolled her eyes. "Really?"

"You looked just like Tansy there for a moment," he told her.

"My granddaughter is a wonderful girl who knows nonsense when she's being fed it." Sonora shook her head. "A fight? Like you want me to call you out for being a cranky bastard or something?"

"I guess." He thought back to the last time she'd given him hell. "You can say I'm an old fool and tell people that I need to grow a sense of humour."

"Oh, trust me, I don't need coaching about what I could complain about where you're concerned." She said it dryly, but her expression grew lighter. "Are you sure you're not making a bigger deal about this than we have to?"

"You want everyone up in our business?" he demanded.

Sonora gave him the stink eye. "We live in a small town, Ashton. Everyone is always up in each other's business."

"Not ours," he pointed out. "Which is why I'm sorry. I must have screwed up. But I think it's easily solved."

She sighed heavily. "Fine. I'll call you a curmudgeon and a pain in the ass, and we'll have everyone talking about how the two of us should never be left alone because we're likely to burn the place down."

Ashton glanced around to be sure no one was close enough to see or hear. Then he crowded forward and pressed her to the wall with his body. "That part is right. The burning the place down."

"Trouble." Sonora caught his face in her hands and kissed him sweetly. Tongue teasing past his lips in a way that made him light up from the inside out.

He leaned their foreheads together. "Can I come over tomorrow?"

She raised a brow. "I'll think about it. I don't know that hanging out with a curmudgeon is what I want."

He snickered. "There's that twenty-five-dollar word again."

"Get used to it." Then she kissed him until he didn't care what she called him.

Although he was more careful and adjusted his expression, and his erection, before he walked into the public area. No need to advertise to everyone exactly how she made him feel.

This thing between them was private, for fuck's sake. Why did anyone else need to go sticking their nose into their business? What they did behind closed doors was for them and them alone.

It's a fine thing, though. Hiding it seems wrong.

Where the thought had come from, he wasn't sure. Ashton gave his head a shake and focused on all the other things he needed to accomplish that day.

Longing for the next moment they could be together.

Sonora didn't like it when she fell into a snit. She was a grown woman, for heaven's sake, and responsible for her own emotions, but for some reason, Ashton's orchestration of the fight scheduled for the following morning had been more than enough to push her into pissed-off territory.

She sat in the most comfortable chair in her living room and brooded.

You're in a mood.

Gah. Couldn't her ghost show up and make distracting conversation? No, he had to refocus her right back on what was pissing her off in the first place.

You're annoying, she mentally told Greg.

You're frustrated. Take it out with something active. Knit, crochet, make Ashton another uber-ugly door decoration. He deserves it.

She laughed. She'd forgotten about the time a few years back when Ashton had gotten high-handed on her, so she'd made him the gaudiest door decoration possible. A lovely memory. Yes, finding ways to poke at the man over the years did help deal with the frustrating moments.

Hmmmm. Good idea.

Sonora slipped to her craft cupboard and grabbed the materials she needed. Half an hour later, she was nearly done with a macramé wall hanging. She'd gone for simple, just a series of knots in a repeating checkerboard style.

She smoothed out the final strands then started another one, amusement rising. The repetitive motion of tying knots allowed her thoughts to drift until it finally dawned on her exactly why she was so annoyed.

Ashton clearly felt it was important to keep them a secret. Which, fine. That's what they'd agreed to, and she didn't really have a problem with it. Just with the sense of urgency he'd shared.

Was she so terrible that he couldn't stand *anyone* knowing they were together?

No. That thought was unkind and over the top. Ashton hadn't meant anything by it except to keep the status quo.

But you'd be okay with things not being so secret anymore, wouldn't you?

This time she didn't bother to tell Greg to shut up. The

truth had been sneaking up on her over the past months, but she didn't have to act on it.

In fact, she had to do the exact opposite.

Ashton was right to stick to their original plan. They'd committed to being friends with benefits, and nothing about that commitment had officially changed.

She smoothed another knot and allowed herself the next confession. She loved her home. Loved that the animal rescue she'd established met a need in Heart Falls, but between the two, chores were getting to be too much for her to handle alone.

She couldn't stay on the land forever. Not without making her children put in time and energy—which they very willingly would. Only that wasn't right. Being on the land was her dream, not theirs. If she couldn't do the work, she didn't deserve to stay.

If Ashton were there to share the load—

No. Absolutely not.

What's more, if that was why these tangled emotions had begun to shift in her, Sonora was going to snip that bud immediately. Ashton was her friend, her lover, not someone who was beholden to her in any way. Certainly not someone who should move in with her just to satisfy some need for companionship and help.

Making him change his life and his commitments to serve her better was out of the question. She wouldn't ask him to do the very thing he'd always said he wanted to avoid.

The fact she'd like to have him around more didn't come into play. Every time they talked, it was clear he wasn't ready to retire. He still felt there was too much to do for Silver Stone.

If he wanted them to stick to the plan, she'd do everything she could to keep him happy.

Which was why she showed up at her granddaughters' coffee shop the next morning as arranged. She dropped her things on one of the small tables at the side of the room before heading to the counter to order.

Tansy smiled widely. "Grandma. You're rarely out this early on a Sunday. Meeting someone?"

"Just me," she shared, kissing Tansy and squeezing her tight. "How are you girls?"

"Good but busy. Can we visit tomorrow or Tuesday?"

"Of course. I'm here for some quiet time in a social setting. All I need is a blueberry crumble muffin and a coffee, please."

"Coming right up. I have one with extra brown sugar that you'd like." Tansy grinned wide then got to work on the order.

Sonora took her things and settled in at her chosen battle station. She pulled out her phone, surprised to see a message from Ashton.

Who knew? The man had actually remembered how to text.

Ashton: *on my way*

She laughed. Thank goodness for time stamps, or she'd have no idea when to expect him.

The message had been sent fifteen minutes earlier, which meant when the door opened and he marched in, she was ready. Sonora kept her gaze on the screen of her phone and debated how much mischief she could get in.

Not too much. And she would play her role since he thought it was important.

That didn't mean she couldn't also have some fun.

She typed quickly.

Sonora: *After this is all over, come to my place. I feel the need to strip you down and ride you like a pony.*

She only hesitated for a split second before hitting send.

He paced past her, a buzz rising from his phone as the message arrived. Keeping from snickering was very, very difficult.

Especially when Ashton placed his order then strode to her table. As they'd agreed, he paused with his hand on the back of the second chair. "Mind if I sit?"

She pulled on her haughtiest expression. "As a matter of fact, I do."

The gentle buzz of conversation in the shop dipped to a mere whisper. While she kept her gaze on Ashton, Sonora swore she felt everyone in the room look their direction.

Ashton frowned. "Really?"

"Really." She picked up her coffee and deliberately took a sip. Then she glanced up as if surprised to find him still there. "Go away, Ashton. I'm trying to enjoy my breakfast. I don't need a curmudgeon like you making my coffee curdle."

He sputtered, eyes flashing at her words. Then he dipped his chin and twisted away. The chair at the next table over was also empty, and he jerked it out, the legs clattering over the wooden floor.

Dropping into the chair as if it were made of concrete instead of metal, Ashton settled with his back to her. He laid his phone on the table. Once he poked at the screen, a sharp inhale followed, and he shot upright, shoulders stiffening.

It appeared he'd spotted her message. Good. This could be fun.

Ashton left his phone faceup on the table, which meant every time she hit Send, the new alert popping up was perfectly visible. Of course, his body language screamed something was going on.

With every uncomfortable shift, Sonora's amusement rose. She also began to feel a little sorry for him—but only a little. He'd asked for her to do exactly what she was doing right now.

Well, not the sexual innuendo. That was fully on her, but she would make it up to him. Eventually.

Ashton's focus alternated between a fixation on his breakfast and staring off into space, trying not to react to her taunting.

Sonora: *Do you remember the time I was behind the desk in your office and had my mouth wrapped around your cock when one of the hands walked in?*

Sonora: *You spilled on my tongue moments after they left.*

Sonora: *We should do that again.*

Sonora: *Soon.*

He groaned. Literally groaned.

Sonora sipped her coffee and pretended to read something on her phone and allowed her amusement to rise. Poor Ashton. What a tangled web. Soothing his ego would come later, but for now, she simply sat there and enjoyed her meal, eavesdropping on nearby conversations.

Beside her, a group of six wonderful young people had gathered. All but one of them were familiar and held a place in her affections. Sonora knew Brooke and Mack the best, Brooke from years together in the community. The others were more recent newcomers, but all of them had firm places in Heart Falls already. Alex worked at Silver Stone with Ashton, and Ryan owned Rough Cut, and both volunteered with the fire department. The young veterinarian, Yvette, was a regular at the animal rescue, and Sonora appreciated her tender heart and technical skills.

The conversation took a turn for the worse when Alex tried for a joke, and it more than fell flat. His comment about taking someone for a ride came out borderline creepy, and Sonora decided now was as good a time as any to get out of the room and save the poor man from himself.

She stood and stepped to the table.

"That was more trouble than it's worth." She glanced disapprovingly at Alex before angling her head until no one else could see her offer him a wink. She turned her gaze on the three women seated at the table. She smiled and held out a hand to the visitor in the group. "Sonora Fallen. If you three would like to go for a ride, I can make that happen."

Ryan's friend, Madison Joy, shook the offered hand and grinned excitedly. "That's wonderful. Thank you."

Yvette continued to peer at Alex with amusement, but she answered Sonora as well. "That is great. Both going for a ride and the fact that Alex feels about *this* big right now."

She held up a finger and thumb as if holding a grain of sand.

Alex looked as contrite as he could under the circumstances. "I apologize. I had about three smart-ass comments that wanted to come out at once, and they tangled together in a bad way."

"Then maybe you should try avoiding smart-assery," Yvette suggested before facing Sonora. "Let's set up a time that works for everyone."

Sonora agreed to meet them in a few days then headed home and put on the kettle.

Sure enough, Ashton showed up twenty minutes later.

She stayed where she was as he settled beside her on the couch. "Do you feel we are sufficiently *not* a couple in the eyes of the community?"

He nodded but caught her fingers in his, gaze unfocused, thoughts obviously elsewhere.

Sonora cupped his face and pulled him toward her. "Talk to me. I'm sorry if I was out of line."

"What?" He blinked in surprise as he pressed a kiss to her palm. "No. You were hysterical, and I didn't mind one bit. Just feeling a little tangled inside."

"About anything in particular?"

He considered. "Seeing Ryan with Madison. It feels as if there's a spark of something there, but I don't want to imagine things where there isn't." Ashton lifted his gaze to hers. "He's a good man who's been lonely for a long time. I compare that to the misery my brother and his wife put each other through daily, and nothing makes sense."

Jeez. His brother's relationship was a land mine Sonora usually chose to ignore. It had become clear over the years that their poor example of a marriage affected Ashton greatly, though.

Still, she could speak about the other part of his comment with authority.

She pressed against Ashton and held on tight. "Death never makes sense. Whether it's friends, like the Stones, or the ones we love heart and soul, like Ryan's Justina or my Greg. Especially when it feels as if you never really got to say goodbye."

Ashton nodded, sorrow in his eyes and a furrow building between his brow.

Sonora smoothed her fingers over the line as she shared, "Ryan and I talked a couple months ago about what it was like to lose someone we loved." She stared at Ashton's hands, noting the strength in them. The scuffed knuckles and the lines that years of hard labour had etched into his skin. "About how some people root themselves into your soul." She stroked Ashton's cheek, thoughts of those they'd lost over the years stirring up bone-deep sadness. "They're still with us in a way, but it's never the same."

"You always love them."

She nodded. "I will love Greg until the day I die. Ryan will love his Justina." The roots of that feeling remained strong inside. Having loved that strongly was a privilege and a curse.

She and Ashton sat in silence for another few minutes before she lifted her face to his. The smart, wonderful man took the hint and kissed her, and all thoughts of the coffee shop, the teasing, the sadness—that vanished as they slipped into giving to each other.

Slow and languid and very, very pleasureful.

HOURS LATER, Sonora stood by the back door and waited as he pulled on his things and prepared to leave. Ashton once again curled his arms around her and held her close before kissing her goodbye. "I'll see you soon."

He was nearly out the door when she remembered. "Wait, I have something for you."

She grabbed the wall hanging and pressed it into his hands.

"What's this?" He unrolled it, his confusion clear as he held the support string and the multitude of cotton knots cascaded down from his fingers.

She smiled sweetly. "It's to brighten up your place. I made it and thought of you." Which wasn't a lie at all.

He cleared his throat, brain obviously in overdrive as he considered his response. "I love it."

How she kept a straight face, she had no idea. "I'm glad."

When Ashton left, she sat down and made five more.

11

As usual, December passed in a rush of family activities and community events. This year there was the added excitement created by Ryan's holiday guest.

The creation of a Not-So-Nutcracker performance had been a moment of brilliance on Madison's part. The community event consumed everyone's imagination and focus for a solid two weeks. Successful as a fundraiser, successful as a lot of fun.

Two evenings after the performance, and two days before Christmas, Sonora dug her hand into the popcorn bowl and burrowed harder against Ashton's side as they sat on her couch to watch the replay that had just been loaded to the cloud.

Ashton's dog, Beauty, lay curled up on the floor at their feet. Such a sweet doggy, really.

"In another part of the barn, the wisest of the creatures joined the dance. Oh, wait. Not the wisest—"

"Get ready, here you come." Sonora poked Ashton.

He folded his arms over his chest and pretended to pout. "I can't believe you convinced people to pony up money for me to be a goat."

"If the beard fits..." She squeaked and wiggled away from

his touch. "Don't tickle. I need to concentrate. Appreciating your performance requires all my attention."

"Fine." Ashton tugged her back into place, amusement in his tone as he chuckled at the antics on the screen. He and his fellow volunteers who had been sponsored to perform as goats kicked up their heels and otherwise cavorted on the stage. Extra-long beards in place, they wore hats with furry ears attached.

For the crowning moment of their time onstage, they all rushed together and pretended to climb onto each other's backs. In reality there was a lot of bending and stretching, so in the end, all five of the "goats" were lined up in a straight vertical line.

"It was a lot of fun," Ashton admitted. "And I'm proud the tower worked. That was my idea," he shared.

"You were just going out of your way to avoid people thinking you're a curmudgeon." She jumped off the couch this time to escape his fingers. "Ashton Stewart. Behave."

He lowered the popcorn bowl to the coffee table and stalked after her, the show forgotten. His gaze grew heated, the warning of pleasure in his eyes. "I think we need to agree to remove that word from the collective memory of the community. It's gotten old."

"Curmudgeon? Really? But it flows off the tongue so smoothly." She dodged to the side, but he caught her, pulling their bodies together. "Curmudg—"

He covered her mouth with his and cut off the teasing.

She reached down and linked their fingers, savouring the kiss, soaking in the connection.

When they broke apart, she asked before assuming. "Are you spending more time with me tonight?"

Ashton motioned for Beauty to stay. The dog stretched, then curled up happily in front of the fire.

Then Ashton focused his attention on Sonora again,

brushing his thumb back and forth over her knuckles as they made their way to the bedroom. "I hoped you'd ask. I booked the morning off as well, so we have all the time we want."

A treat, to be sure. Especially considering they'd likely not see each other until January with how busy Christmas Day and the rest of the year usually got.

A thought that had been teasing her over the past weeks finally prodded hard enough that Sonora took the chance. Simply sliding into bed would be easy, but they were good enough friends that the question needed to be asked. "You made any plans for the new year?"

"Like resolutions?" Ashton sat on the bed and pulled her between his spread legs. He grimaced, rose briefly, then pulled his phone from his back pocket and dropped it beside his hips. "I try to avoid those. Never last for long, anyway."

"I was thinking more about your workload. You are going to celebrate your sixty-fifth birthday soon. Any thoughts about slowing down? Making eventual plans for some sort of retirement?"

"Thought about it," Ashton admitted. "Sometimes I think I'm still trying to live up to that promise I made Walter to be there for his kids."

She stilled. "Oh, Ashton."

"The man was one of my best friends." He shook his head. "Still one of my best friends. I swear I hear his voice at times. He tells me what needs to be looked at or jabs me with new ideas to share with Caleb and the other boys." Ashton made a face. "That probably sounds as if I'm not all there. Voices in my head…"

"Oh, I don't think it's strange at all," Sonora assured him dryly.

She ignored the faint chuckle of amusement from her own ghostly companion.

Ashton snorted softly. "Listen to me. Caleb and the rest of

them are all over thirty years old, and I still call them *boys*." He met her gaze. "I know I'm getting older. The days keep getting longer, and the cold is sharper than ever. The bales are heavier, and sunup comes far too early. But I promised I'd be there for them, Sonora. They still need a foreman who knows the place. Someone needs to deal with all the fiddly details so they can concentrate on the important ones and be there for each other."

She couldn't fault him for caring so deeply. But she could try to remind him to care for himself as well.

"They do need you, but they don't need you full time," she suggested. "Also, Walter himself would be the first to tell you that you deserve to enjoy life more. Same as you tell the *boys*." She said the last word with emphasis, and he laughed.

"I suppose." He folded his arms over his chest.

Sonora knew that look. "You plan to simply ignore this conversation, don't you? Nothing will change if you don't put the wheels in motion."

"I will. I will," Ashton grumbled. "But not now. It's the holidays. Just leave things alone. It's too much to deal with changes as well as the rest of it."

Sonora spoke softly, but she could be persistent if necessary. "It's not that hard, you know. Asking for help. Doing the next thing that needs to be done."

He glared at her. "Now you're talking nonsense."

"Really, I'm not." How to explain it to the stubborn man when he wasn't listening? "What if you asked Tucker to come apprentice with you? Your nephew would love to return to Silver Stone. He's got friends and family here. He'd be perfect. Now and in the future."

"I can't ask him to leave his job and come work for me."

"Why ever not?" Sonora planted her fists on her hips. "If you ask me, he'd choose you and Silver Stone over some random horse stable if he got the chance."

"Right. Fine. I'll call him. After the holidays," Ashton added.

"Why are you making this harder than it should be?" Sonora demanded. "At least send him a text and ask him to consider it. That'll give him time to decide and possibly deal with his current position."

"A text?"

She threw her hands in the air, frustration finally breaking through and stealing her calm. She grabbed his phone from where it rested beside his hips and shook it at him. "Join the current world. People like texting, Ashton. Heck, if you don't want to type it yourself, you can even get your phone to do it. Just say, 'Siri, text Tucker.'"

"Then what? 'Hey, I need you. Get your ass here as soon as possible'?" Ashton stood as he pulled the phone from her fingers and tossed it into the chair beside the bed. "He's a grown man, Sonora. I can't order him around."

"Well, I'm a grown woman, and you have zero trouble trying to order me around."

Ashton caught her by the hand and tugged her hard against his body. "You like it when I get bossy."

"Usually," she admitted. "But if this part of the conversation is your idea of foreplay, you've got another think coming."

He stroked a thumb over her bottom lip. Slowing the motion, he caressed and stroked until she relaxed against him. He raised a brow. "You know, your expression a few minutes ago could have flayed the skin off a tough old boar."

She looked him up and down. "Didn't work."

He snickered. "Damn, you kill me, woman."

"Only in my dreams, darling," she said cheerily, even as she pulled her attitude back into line. "I'm sorry. I dug into your business harder than I should have. As a friend, I care about you, and I want to see you enjoying yourself and staying healthy."

"I heard the sentiment behind the prodding," Ashton assured her. He stroked a hand up her body. "Apology accepted. We should have some make-up sex."

She laughed. "How is make-up sex different from the other sex we enjoy?"

"Well…" He slipped her loose T-shirt up and over her head, gaze drifting along her skin like a caress. As he spoke, he traced the outline of the vine on her hip. "It's not as fast and furious as sex against the wall in the tack room. And less athletic than sex in the tractor, which is good, because I think I can only bend that way once in my lifetime."

Amused, Sonora tugged off his shirt so she could rub her palms over his warm, muscular shoulders. "So far, you're telling me what it's not. How about what it is?"

"Slow." He pulled her close and pressed a kiss between her breasts as he reached behind her and undid her bra. "With kisses everywhere until you're melting in my arms. Until you're liquid around my cock. Breathless as you call out my name."

Whoa. She let her head fall back as he wrapped his lips around her nipple and teased the tip. "Okay."

He smiled, the motion tugging her skin. "Okay," he agreed.

Sonora breathed deep and let him take control.

Ashton opened his eyes to a warm woman curled against him, the lights on her Christmas tree twinkling with a glow like old-fashioned candles.

He stroked her skin, savouring the heat. "Morning. You awake?"

She laughed softly. "Silliest question ever."

"Let me rephrase. You sleep well?"

She pressed a kiss to his chest, hand pressed over his heart. "Slept long and hard, and no jokes. I'm feeling very happy and relaxed, and I don't want anything to intrude and spoil the moment."

The night before had been a balancing act, so he agreed. They hadn't come to any solutions—

They were good at not coming to solutions, it seemed.

"I'll give it more thought," he promised. "About getting Tucker to come help."

She nodded. "Want some coffee? Breakfast? Or are you headed to the chow line at Silver Stone?"

He rolled her on top, smiling with contentment as her silver-grey hair showered over them. "I'm taking the morning off, remember?"

Her smile was bright in return.

Hours later, Ashton whistled as he got back to work, not even caring who might hear him as he entered the barns at Silver Stone after lunch.

"Ashton. Goddamn it."

Contentment vanished as Luke shouted in his face.

Ashton jerked to a stop. What the hell? "Luke? You lost your mind?"

"Where the hell have you been?" Luke looked him up and down, dragging a hand through his hair. "Wait, I have to let the others know you're okay."

"The others?"

Luke hauled out his phone, fingers flying over the screen before burning Ashton with the full weight of his glare. "You sent Tucker a damn SOS, and then no one could find you. We've been worried sick. You weren't answering your phone, so we called all your friends, but no one had any idea where you were."

"I took the morning off. It was on the schedule," Ashton insisted.

A huge sigh escaped Luke. "It was, but dammit, Ashton. You need to get with the program in terms of technology. For some God-awful reason, your phone sent through a text at three a.m. You scared the daylights out of Tucker. And the rest of us."

"I have my phone set to Do Not Disturb between midnight and six. But you and Caleb and a few others can always reach me." Ashton insisted.

Luke held out his hand toward Ashton. "Give it to me."

Feeling like a rebuked child, Ashton fished his phone out of his pocket.

The younger man checked a few tabs then offered Ashton a long-suffering sigh. He held up the phone and pointed to the side of it. "Ringer. Up is on, down is off."

"Fuck." Ashton was horrified that he'd put them all through that stress. "Tucker?"

"Is on his way." Luke shrugged. "Call him. I sent a general message that you're okay, but you should follow up."

"Will do." Ashton laid a hand on Luke's arm. "Sorry. I know you have your friends arriving today."

"And my sister is coming home too," Luke reminded him before rolling his eyes and waving Ashton's apologies off. "It's all good. Come on—we've got chores to get done. The foreman around here is a real hard-ass."

Ashton laughed, but he held up his phone. "I'll be right there. I should let Tucker shout at me first."

Luke patted him on the back then marched into the barn.

There wasn't as much shouting as Ashton would have imagined, but a whole lot of sighing and complaining about technology and boomers.

"I'm on the way already, so I'll just come for a few days," Tucker said.

"Come for as long as you can," Ashton suggested. "We have a lot to catch up on, and it'd be good to have you around."

Good to maybe have a conversation about being around so Ashton could ease into something different.

It was a good thing chores were repetitive, muscle-burning tasks, because Ashton's brain went into overdrive. He hauled bales until his arms shook with fatigue, but he still couldn't quite get his thoughts to line up properly.

Did he want to retire?

No. He wasn't ready for that, but he could handle some adjustments to his daily routine.

Images flooded his mind.

An alarm clock showing eight o'clock and Ashton lingering over coffee.

A warm fireplace with Sonora sitting in the chair beside him. Or better yet, on the couch with him, bodies touching as they listened to music and enjoyed an evening together.

Him driving out to spend the evening with his friends, Sonora waving him off.

His friends teasing as he prepared to head home, Gary and James razzing him about the warm woman he was eager to return to...

Ashton dropped the bale in his hands and shot upright. *Fuck.*

Those weren't daydreams about semiretirement. Well, okay, some of them were. But the common factor—the part that absolutely wasn't true right now?

Sonora in his life and everyone knowing it. Accepting it.

Honouring this thing between them.

Ashton collapsed onto the nearest bale and stared into the distance. That...

That wasn't what Sonora had agreed to. Which made sense, because it hadn't been what they'd been looking for when they'd started as lovers.

What they were doing—what they had been doing for the past year—there was nothing wrong in it. But things had changed. He'd changed.

Hadn't he?

It was a good thing that there were a ton of people around and a lot to do because Ashton stumbled through the next hours without needing to engage much brain power.

Tucker arrived. His nephew smacked him on the back then hugged the hell out of him. "I'm glad you're not dead, but if you ever do that to me again, I'll kill you."

Ashton laughed. "I'm sorry. Just take my phone away."

"No, what we're going to do is give you lessons on how to actually use it."

Damn. "Now, that's fighting dirty."

Tucker grinned. "Show me around for a few hours. I'll need to hit the sack early. Three a.m. was two time zones away and a long time ago."

"If you're trying to make me feel guilty, it's working," Ashton complained.

"Good." Tucker stepped back in time to avoid Ashton's fist. "How about a ride first? Let me work out the traveling kinks before we start the tour."

The ride took a couple of hours. Ashton enjoyed the time shooting the breeze with his nephew. They visited all the old haunts Tucker wanted to see, like the viewpoint for Heart Falls and the spot where a young Luke and Tucker had attempted to build a tree house.

The visit turned into dinner in the mess hall, and then Tucker vanished into one of the trailers for the night.

Which meant Ashton was alone in his quarters before ten p.m. with far too much to think about.

This thing he had going with Sonora was good. No—it was great.

It was also terrible because the sex-only secret arrangement was rapidly becoming not enough, but damn if Ashton knew what to do about it.

He thought about what she'd shared just the other night. About how losing someone you loved never faded.

She still loved Greg.

A rush of emotion swamped him, and he was shocked to discover the primary sentiment was jealousy.

Goddammit. He was jealous of a dead man.

Ashton dragged a hand through his hair and called himself twelve kinds of asshole. He shoved to his feet and paced the distance between his bedroom and kitchen, frustration rising.

Of course Sonora still loved Greg. The man had been her first love. They'd worked together and raised a child. Time would have no reason to fade the depth of that caring.

Heck, Ashton would have to say that after nearly fourteen years of them being gone, he still loved the Stones, and that had been in a completely platonic, friends-only way. Sonora and Greg had shared intimacy—

Ashton shoved away the heated pain that struck. Yeah. Jealousy was the only word for it, as much as he hated to admit it.

Tonight he wished with everything in him that he was still needed at the Stone house. Putting up decorations and preparing the house for Christmas morning would have been a welcome distraction.

Instead he was stuck with his own thoughts and his own demons.

So he went back to his usual solution for when he needed to think. Pulled on a coat and made his way back to the barn. If Happy-Go-Lucky was surprised to see him show up, the horse didn't care, just happily leaned into Ashton's touch as he dragged the brush over his flanks.

Patient creature.

It was late by the time Ashton hauled himself to bed, no

solution in mind. Even while joining the Stones for dinner on Christmas Day as tradition called for, he spent more time worrying over the problem than being present.

Thankfully, Caleb shared the wonderful news that Silver Stone's finances were not just good but rock-solid. Things could change in all the right ways.

And the ideas Ashton had been futilely chasing since the previous day fell into place.

He hauled Tucker back to his rooms, ready to drop the bomb. It took a few minutes to get there, but the moment he could finally say it, it was a relief like nothing he'd felt before.

"Since I know you like to have things plotted out well in advance, an annoying habit you got from your parents that has persisted in spite of all my attempts to break you of it, bust out your spreadsheets and get working on this." Ashton met his nephew's gaze straight on. "You're right. I am interested in Sonora"—he raised a finger in warning—"and you are not to repeat that to *anyone*. But that means at some point I want to be ready to do the next thing."

"Makes sense. What does that have to do with me?"

Ashton let the words spill free. "I want you ready to take over as foreman when the time comes."

It might have been silly of him to have needed Sonora's prompting a few days ago to get here, but now that he had seen a glimpse of the future, it made perfect sense.

Ashton plotted and planned with Tucker for another hour before his nephew pled exhaustion and disappeared for the evening.

Unlike the previous night, Ashton felt filled with energy and hope. It wasn't going to be easy making a shift. He would have to be very, very patient and very convincing.

And smart. The last thing he wanted to do was chase Sonora away with his demands. She might not mind him being bossy during sex, but she'd made it crystal clear that bossing her around in real life was an absolute no.

Ashton stared around the walls of his living room and eyed the macramé on display. Rainbow colours, some pure white. In the three weeks since she'd given him the first one, two dozen more had been added. He knew damn well Sonora was getting some kind of perverse pleasure out of making them for him.

Who was he to tell her no?

But as he gathered them up to move them to a new location, one by one, he made plans.

12

———————

It wasn't easy to give a man who had pretty much everything he wanted—and simple tastes to boot— what he wanted for his birthday. Especially when his nephew and the other men in his life organized a surprise birthday party and planned to whisk Ashton away without sharing said details of whisking with her.

How rude. Sonora couldn't fathom why she wasn't simply cc'd on every decision related to the man. It would certainly have made her life easier.

She chuckled even as she eyed the calendar and tried to decide the solution to her dilemma.

You could crash the party.

Greg's ghostly suggestion made her fold her arms and glare at the calendar even harder. "Right, no. Last information I got out of Walker, there will be more than twenty guys at the event. I'm sure me showing up would mess up the *we're just grumpy friends* ploy."

You're not crashing the party for their sake but for Ashton's.

"Ashton can get his present later. It's not as if the actual day is magic or anything."

I bet he'd like his present on the actual day.

"You're annoying, as usual," she told Greg. "Of course Ashton would like me to come and sex him up on his birthday. He'd like me to come sex him up every day if it worked."

She paused. Well, maybe that wasn't true. Their continued exploits were still entertaining and enthusiastic, but they were no longer as regular as they had been.

In fact, entire weeks had begun to pass between getting-naked events. The strangest thing was she hadn't really noticed, which made her all kinds of dumbfounded.

Not that she'd overlooked the lack of naked time, but they'd always seemed to have something else they needed to do more.

Sometimes they ended up on the couch, talking through things that had happened at Silver Stone. Or when she'd had issues come up with the animal shelter and needed to make plans for the best way to move ahead, they'd brainstormed ideas together.

Stripping down after those moments hadn't felt necessary. Spending time together had been enjoyable in an entirely different way. She wasn't about to complain about that.

On the downside, less sex meant Ashton seemed to have more time and energy to get in trouble. Over the past weeks, he'd annoyed her twice without even trying.

Or maybe he was trying and simply being truly successful.

First, she'd found out he'd put in an order for the animal shelter using Silver Stone's connections. Which was sweet of him and a potential money saver, only she'd already committed resources and ended up having to juggle with the bank to make things balance.

Then, early in the month, she'd opened her door to discover Brooke Klassen standing there with a huge smile, her husband waving from the parking area.

"Just grabbing your keys," Brooke offered, hand outstretched.

Sonora eyed her with confusion. "My keys?"

"Yup. I'll drive her."

Part of their conversation seemed to be missing. Sonora tried again. "You want my keys." She peered around Brooke at Mack, who sat behind the wheel of their truck. "Is there something wrong with yours? I don't mind lending you my ride, but—"

"Oh, no. Sorry. I thought you knew. Ashton arranged with Dad and I to do a tune-up and tire check for you. I can sneak you in today and be done by Wednesday."

Sonora held her tongue. She wasn't about to take it out on Brooke that the timing wasn't great. Sonora was due in town on Tuesday. She'd have to ask one of the girls to come and get her, which she hated to do on their day off.

Still, she could roll with the punches.

"Let me grab them," Sonora offered.

"No problem." Brooke rubbed her arms over her coat. "It's cold this morning."

"Good thing neither of us has to work outside. I count my blessings every day." Sonora dropped the keys into Brooke's hand. "You and Mack want to come for dinner this week?"

"I'd like that," Brooke said. "We've been doing renovations on the house, and getting away from the mess would be a nice change."

Plans arranged, Sonora waved goodbye then closed the door and let a huge sigh escape.

She wasn't sure what to do. Send Ashton a message saying, *Thank you for helping take care of my truck?* Or curse him out and smack him with a *don't ever schedule something for me without asking again* warning?

She liked that he had thought to help her. She did.

Sonora returned to her spot in front of the fire and decided no response was probably the right response.

Frustrating man.

A week later, with her truck back where it belonged, Sonora faced a new dilemma. Despite his mistakes over the past couple of weeks, today was Ashton's birthday. Celebrating birthdays was a lifetime rule, and she wasn't going to mess with that habit now.

Especially since sixty-five was a milestone, and they had been doing this friendship thing for years and years. So what if the surprise party Tucker had organized for his uncle made delivering Ashton's present a little harder than usual? She liked a challenge.

She needed help, though. The logistics were too much otherwise.

~

SONORA PULLED around the side of the house into the space next to Lisa and Josiah's family SUV. It was early enough that Josiah was still at work doing veterinarian stuff, and the rest of the birthday attendees were nowhere near.

Lisa? She knew how to keep her mouth shut.

Sonora made her way to the back door and let herself in. "Lisa?"

"In here."

Kids' music played merrily in the background, and childish laughter and chatter guided Sonora to the family room, where Lisa was supervising her daughter, Zoë, and her nephew, Tyler. The toddlers were both under three and obviously close friends as well as family.

Until Zoë stole a truck right out of Tyler's fingers, and he hollered his disapproval.

"Welcome to chaos," Lisa offered Sonora with a laugh. "Zoë. Sharing does not mean you get to *take* the toy from your cousin. Give it back."

Sonora watched with amusement as Lisa patiently dealt

with the babies. "I don't want to take you from your entertainment."

"You're welcome to head out to the playhouse to do whatever you need to do. I hauled the air mattress out this morning and covered it with sheets. Also, there's an electric heater on the shelf. Just turn it off when you're done." Lisa mimed putting a key to her lips and twisting it. "I swear I know nothing."

Sonora leaned down and kissed Lisa's forehead. The young woman had become a good friend over the past couple of years. She was also whip smart and somehow seemed to have the pulse on every bit of gossip in the community.

Lisa having already discovered what Sonora and Ashton were doing was a foregone conclusion. "The truth is you know everything, sweetheart. And I like you that way."

"I just hope I'm pulling tricks like this when I'm sixty." Lisa grinned. "Actually, *Josiah* hopes I'm pulling tricks like this when I'm sixty."

Laughter spilled free as Sonora left the room and went to make the final preparations.

Returning to the scene of the crime that evening, Sonora took a deep breath then carefully made her way to the playhouse. She stuck to the shadows the best she could until it was just a short dash up the ramp into the playhouse. The crusted snow underfoot held her up but crunched with each step, and the temperature seemed to drop with every step she took. As she hurried through the dark backyard, the robe she'd pulled around her torso fluttered in the wind.

It was cold as the devil. Thank goodness for the heater out in the playhouse and the electric blanket getting a workout.

Sonora set a match to the candle in the window then reached for her phone. Now for the tricky part. What if Ashton had left *his* phone at home? What if he simply didn't answer?

The truth was if all her efforts failed tonight, Sonora didn't mind one bit. The goal was for Ashton to have a wonderful evening. If that happened without her help, so be it.

She typed her message then crossed her fingers and hit Send.

Sonora: *Happy birthday. Having fun?*

ASHTON HAD ONLY INTENDED to walk away from his party for a few minutes, but after seeing a mysterious form race across the backyard, he'd been too curious to resist checking it out.

The wood creaked underfoot as he made his way up the ramp to the playhouse Josiah Ryder had built in his backyard. As far as forts went, it was a fine one, with real windows and a door that Ashton pushed forward to discover Sonora bundled in a blanket, gaze snapping off her phone to meet his.

"Sonora? What the hell?"

Her amusement was all too clear. "Well, I sure hope I get that quick a response the next time I text."

Ashton closed the door, ducking slightly as he did so. Surprisingly, there was heat in the small space, which confused him even further. "What are you doing here?"

The small eight-by-eight-foot space was mostly filled by what seemed to be an air mattress and tons of pillows and blankets.

Sonora caught his hand. "Waiting to give you your birthday present."

She tugged. The unexpected move dropped him to his knees on the air mattress, rocking slightly as he fought for balance.

"*Sonora.*"

A quick push on his shoulders put him flat on his back. A moment later, she'd straddled his hips.

Okay, he liked this. Liked it a lot.

The expression she wore when she was up to trouble slipped into place, familiar and welcome. "I know. You're having a birthday party with your friends. Far be it from me to disturb you."

He laughed, instinctively palming her hips. "The fact you're here, with what seems to be a bed and questionable intentions, is the straight-up definition of disturbing me."

The sweet, tempting woman pressed her hands to his chest and leaned closer. Her long hair fell around her face, pretty as a picture as he gazed into her laughing eyes. Her lips inches from his, she hummed happily. "*Questionable* intentions? I'd hope they were pretty clear."

Ashton slid a hand up her back to tangle his fingers in her hair. One small tug and he'd adjusted the angle so he could kiss her. Lips firm against hers as he took control. The heat between them was intense and quick to rise as always.

He rolled, sliding her under him and settling between her thighs. The air mattress wiggled slightly, but it was firm enough for their purposes here and now. Warmth wrapped around them, gliding from the heater in the corner of the small space.

There was no mistaking what Sonora wanted, and maybe he was a bastard for being willing to ignore his friends for a time to accept her gift.

Sonora licked her lips, and any intentions he had of doing the honorable thing and asking for a rain check vanished in a blaze of heat and need.

SHE WAS SUPPOSED to be the one seducing him, but suddenly, she was the one being enticed deeper. Drawn with each motion of his lips against hers to connect more fully.

To taste him, to accept him. To savour the hunger in his

touch as he braced himself on one arm and smiled down at her with sin in his eyes.

Ashton's fingers on the belt of her robe moved with such talent, Sonora's amusement rose as well. "You're very good at that."

"Practice makes perfect. God, woman. What you do to me." He pushed aside the fabric and cupped one big palm over her breast, staring down as if he'd uncovered a masterpiece.

Him looking at her that way made her feel treasured. Always had.

Sonora threaded her fingers through his hair, stroking his shoulders, reaching to caress his back. He kissed his way down her body, and it wasn't where she'd planned the adventure to go, but moving him from his path was impossible.

"I'm supposed to give *you* a present," she complained before gasping. He'd slipped a hand into her panties and unerringly found the perfect spot to send her pleasure skyward.

"I have my present," Ashton said. "It's perfect. Not quite the right colour, though."

She examined his face in confusion.

Ashton jerked her panties off then resumed his position between her thighs. "Yup, I like it when things are a little rosier, don't you?"

He cupped his hands under her butt and lifted her sex to his mouth, hungrily taking her higher with each lick of his tongue over her clit, each stroke through her folds, each plunge into her core—each one perfect and dragging an uncontrollable response from her body.

"Sweet Sonora," Ashton breathed against her, the heat of his breath caressing the wetness he'd created. "I love how you taste. How you soak my fingers and squeeze me tight. I want you molten before you slide around my cock."

"Keep talking," Sonora begged before deciding that was a terrible idea. "No, stop talking and use your tongue. Please."

He laughed, teasing her with the scruff on his chin. Brushing the rough texture slowly over the skin he'd made so sensitive with his kiss, he made the reaction skitter through to her scalp.

Then he lowered his mouth over her again, sliding fingers into her core. Drawing them out slowly, easing back in. Over and over, until she was breathless, her chest rocking as she reached for release.

"Ashton." A command? A request, maybe.

He took it as a call to action. He rose over her and freed his cock. Fingers between her thighs, he guided the tip into her heat.

Sonora widened her thighs, welcoming him in. Thankfully, they had no need of condoms anymore. No need to waste time juggling that complication. She cupped his face in her hands and stared into his eyes.

He pushed home with one firm motion.

She closed her eyes, amazed as always at how good it felt to fit together. To have him inside her, hot and hard and perfect. Sonora wrapped her fingers around his biceps and stroked the hard muscles. His flannel shirt soft against her fingertips, and beneath it, the strength of him there in every movement.

In the way he held himself over her, braced on one arm. The way he kept his other hand between them, sliding wetness from her core over her clit.

With each thrust of his hips, his fingers slicked the sensitive nerves, and the orgasm that had faded slightly reared again, nearly breaking free.

This thing between them was good. So very good, how could she not simply want this?

"Harder." Sonora dug her fingernails in and held on.

He cursed softly but increased his pace. The rock-hard muscles of his butt clenched as he drove his hips forward. His breath escaped in sharp gasps, and fiery desire painted his features.

The rapid pace was enough to start the spiral, his hardness inside her stroking all the right spots. Add in his fingers on her clit, and Sonora was gone.

"Ashton."

She gasped his name as her sex contracted around him. He instantly slowed, not breaking her pleasure but prolonging it. Needy sounds slipped free as Ashton stroked in and out with the rhythm of her pulsing core, sending a fresh rush of pleasure through her over and over.

He lasted a dozen movements past her release, driving deep and holding himself there as his arms shook and his hips quivered.

Sonora couldn't open her eyes. She was a melted ice cream cone on a summer day, all spread thin and sweetly messy. "I'm never moving again."

Ashton withdrew with a groan then settled at her side, pulling her against him. He tugged the edges of her robe over her body then tucked her head under his chin. "You might find living in the playhouse a little awkward."

"Worth it," she whispered. Silence surrounded them. Sonora gently patted his chest under her fingers. "Happy birthday."

He was quiet for a moment before pressing his lips to her forehead. "Thank you for my present. It's exactly what I wanted."

Under her palms, his heart beat in a steady rhythm.

She took a deep breath and made the words solid and true. "You're an easy man to make happy. It helps that we've been doing this for a while. We've got enjoying and sharing with each other down pat. No other expectations, no other people in the way. Just us, like we promised."

As sad as that thought now made her.

Ashton stilled. He stayed motionless for longer than expected then finally dipped his chin. "Right. Like we promised."

Five minutes later they were both dressed.

After one final kiss, he returned to his birthday party.

Sonora gathered her things into neat bundles to collect the following day then slipped silently across the yard to where she'd left her truck.

On the drive home, she alternated between smiling and feeling something was slightly off. It had been a good night; she was sure of it. She curled up in her bed at the house, lingering over the sense of contentment at having brought Ashton joy.

She woke the next day with a clouded brain and faint hints of a lingering nightmare. Something that involved empty houses filled with sorrowful ghosts, all of them crying as if their hearts were breaking.

13

September, current year

Sweet, wonderful Sonora Fallen was driving him up the wall.

Ashton had tried everything he could over the past months to ease them into a new stage of their relationship, but none of it seemed to work.

It hadn't only been a refusal on her part, he had to admit. The entire world had conspired to make doing the next thing damn near impossible. Silver Stone had more than a few emergencies, and Tucker had required guidance as he grew into his new role as assistant foreman.

There had been good family events and friends who asked for help, and Ashton considered each of those a privilege and a responsibility.

At this point, patience might be a virtue, but his was wearing thin.

Still, sitting across the table from Gary at Longhorn's was something to be celebrated.

Ashton raised his glass in the air. "To your clean bill of health."

Gary breathed in deep before allowing his shoulders to relax and a smile to rise. "To you, who held my hand through too many fucked-up days of worrying and through doctor's appointments and cancer treatments."

The out-of-the-blue cancer diagnosis had thrown Gary for a loop. Thankfully, the bladder cancer had been caught early, and treatment had gone well. But months had passed in a blur while they did the next thing.

Being here, celebrating life, was important.

"We're friends. I'll always be there for you in the tough moments as well as the easy ones," Ashton told him. "But you're welcome."

Two oversized steaks arrived, and the next moments were about the logistics of diving into the wonderful thank-you meal Gary had organized.

Gary hummed happily around his mouthful of steak then shook his fork at Ashton. "Sonora would love the lake trout. It's only on the menu for the next couple weeks, though."

Ashton nodded. He'd finally confessed his goals regarding Sonora in June, and since then Gary had tried his best to not only be supportive but also offer all sorts of dating advice.

His friend stared at him for a moment before shaking his head. "Have you even asked her yet? Like on a real date?"

"I have," Ashton answered honestly. "She was busy."

Gary raised a brow. "Let me get this straight. You said to her, 'Sonora, I'd like to take you to Longview's for dinner. Let's go on Wednesday.' And then she said no."

"Yes. And no."

"For fuck's sake." Gary leaned his elbows on the table. "Explain."

"I said, 'There's trout on the menu at Longview.' She said, 'That's wonderful news.' And then we had sex."

Gary hung his head, cradling it in his hands. His shoulders rocked, and when he lifted his gaze to Ashton's, amusement flashed but also something else. "You do realize that phrase makes me simultaneously want to cheer for you and punch you in the face."

"Wonderful news?"

"'We had sex,'" Gary returned.

A passing busboy's eyes widened, and Ashton laughed at his friend's horrified expression.

Gary cleared his throat and lowered his voice. "I mean, *you had sex*, with Sonora. Because while I'm happy you're still burning up the sheets, don't you think it's time you moved on?"

"I'm trying," Ashton insisted. "It's been—"

His explanation stalled out. No way would he give even the slightest hint that giving time to Gary had been a chore.

Or giving time to Silver Stone.

To Caleb, to Walker. To Tucker.

There had been small yet important things taking place throughout the year, and Ashton was very happy to have been a part of each. Building an addition on Walker and Ivy's home in preparation for their family adoption. Helping Caleb's oldest daughter, Sasha, strengthen her horse skills. Spending time with Kelli's grandfather, who had taken to visiting the ranch on a regular basis.

Ashton met his friend's gaze straight on and said it clearly. "Sonora and I are friends and have been for a long time. If it takes a little longer to move to the next thing, then so be it. In the meantime, we're still doing what makes us happy. Trust me on that. I'm absolutely committed to being there for her."

Gary sighed but nodded. "I know. And damn, I'm the last man who should try to give you relationship advice. My daughter's mom didn't stick around long enough to see Brooke start school, so this is more about me wanting you to be happy."

"And I am," Ashton offered.

His friend broke into a grin. "God, we're not nearly drunk enough for this conversation."

"Right?" Ashton laid a hand on Gary's shoulder and squeezed. "You're buying me dessert, yes? To make up for all this sticky-sweet emotional shit."

"Absolutely."

Only, on the way out the door, it was Ashton who spoke with the waitress and arranged for a chocolate crème brûlée in a to-go box.

After he dropped Gary at the shop, Ashton made his way to Sonora's.

The sky was alive with a multilayered assortment of colours, sunset painting the clouds overhead gold and red as the sun dropped behind the mountains.

He walked to the porch swing he'd put up for her a year ago. Sonora was stretched out on the platform, swaying gently in the evening breeze.

"Hey."

He settled beside her and kissed her cheek. "Brought you a present."

She eagerly opened the box. "Oh my. Did you hear my sweet tooth singing all the way from the restaurant?"

"You always have a sweet tooth," he said. Then he pulled out the fork he'd hidden in his pocket and offered it to her as well.

Her smile rivaled the bright sky. "Share?"

"Of course." Ashton opened his mouth obediently as she offered the first taste. Sweetness rolled over his tongue, but for every bite he consumed, it was her taste he craved. Her tongue licking the prongs on the fork and her hum of approval as she closed her eyes and swallowed slowly only increased his desire.

He craved not only her touch but *her*.

Ashton took the empty box from her hands and placed it on the ground beside the swing. Then he curled his arm around her as she pressed to his side, gazing over the distant mountains.

He should say something. Tell her how important she was to him. Tell her that he wanted her to make him gaudy macramé and scold him for working too hard.

But when she sighed and pressed a hand to his cheek, he just couldn't. Couldn't break this perfect equilibrium between them that let them be exactly who they were. No hard edges, no compromises or unkindness or awkward decisions. Just Sonora. Just Ashton.

"So beautiful," Sonora said softly. She linked her fingers with his and stared at the darkening sky.

"Very beautiful." Ashton gazed at her and hoped for a miracle. For some wisdom or courage or *something* that would allow him to let go of his fears and finally get this right.

FALL WAS GONE in a blaze of yellow and red, the Alberta temperatures for once dropping hard and fast enough to make the leaves change colour instead of going straight from green to brown and on the ground.

After a few glorious weeks, winter snuck in softer than usual. Freezing temperatures, only a little snow. The landscape everywhere turned into a blur of brown and grey.

When snow finally arrived, it was a relief. Sonora began to prepare for the busyness of the holiday season. Between her family and the animal rescue, there was always enough to distract her.

Also, Ashton. Just...Ashton.

If anything had been a constant this past year, it was that

he'd been on her mind a lot. He'd been in her bed but not necessarily around as much as the previous year.

If you're about to complain Ashton hasn't been around much, you might want to see the time chart I made. Of actual reality versus what you think is real.

Sonora stopped dead in her tracks, glancing around and wishing Greg had a corporeal body she could hit. "A chart?"

Of how much time you spend together.

She could not believe this. "It's bad enough you hang around and speak openly about all the things I'd prefer to ignore, but mentioning charts is beyond the pale."

Her ghost was clearly amused. *Never got over your fear of math, did you, sweetheart?*

Fine. She and Ashton spent plenty of time together. In spite of them both being very busy people, they did things together like chat and fool around and relax.

The sense of something being out of whack, though, had continued to grow. She'd written it off for a while as him working through his fears for Gary. But recently, she'd seen something in Ashton's gaze that made her wonder if they were headed toward the end.

He was quieter. More thoughtful.

She could hardly have any regrets about their past, but the idea of not getting to be with him…

It hurt.

Still, when he showed up at her house on the first Saturday of December, she was willing to push aside her own fears and accept the needy kiss he pressed to her lips.

He broke away, stroking his fingers over her cheek. "Sorry. Should have asked first if you've got plans."

She thought she heard something in the distance, but his hands were on her, and she couldn't concentrate. Couldn't really care that she'd lost all resolve because she wanted this. Wanted him again.

It appeared she was a glutton for punishment. If he had plans for them to slow down, cool off, change course—none of those ideas remotely mattered.

Sonora lifted her lips to his and took the kiss. Took the passion and the pleasure and the connection and pushed away the worries and fears.

Right now, this moment. This place was all they had, and she was going to take it.

Talented hands roamed her body with a knowledge built on years of experience.

He got her unbuttoned, kissing along the edge of her bra. "Can never decide which I like better. You naked in my bed and all the time in the world for just us or these moments when I can't get enough of you fast enough."

"Both." Sonora barely got the word out before she gasped as his teeth grazed the tip of her nipple through her bra.

A *bang*, *bang*, *bang* sounded on the front door.

Sonora cursed. Ashton cursed. They both snickered, even as they separated.

"Door locked?" Ashton whispered, his hot gaze still locked on her torso.

The front of her shirt hung open, skin bared to him. She answered in the same low tone. "Yes."

"Then come here," he growled, tugging her toward him.

Torn between ignoring whoever was outside and wondering if this was an angel rescuing her from a moment of folly, Sonora glanced out the window. "I'm the only one around for the animal shelter. I need to answer it."

Ashton groaned, but he released her. "Fine. But make them go away quickly. I'll wait for you in the bedroom."

His phone rang, and he cursed. He hauled it out of his pocket and turned off the ringer as quickly as possible as he eyed the messages now popping up on the screen.

"Work?"

"Caleb," Ashton whispered. "Shit. He needs me at the stables."

"I'll distract whoever is at the door so you can leave." Maybe it was for the best. Taking a breather might mean time to get her head on straight before they dug this pit any deeper. She twisted toward the door and called out loudly, "Just a minute."

He frowned, all options taken away in that moment. He adjusted his pants and tucked in his shirt as he spoke. "Fine. But call me when you can."

"Of course."

With Ashton headed toward the back door and his boots, Sonora hurriedly went about putting herself back together. She buttoned her shirt and pulled her hair into a messy bun.

A quick peek in the front hall mirror reflected too-bright eyes and very flushed cheeks, but she would have to do. She glanced over her shoulder to make sure Ashton was out the back door.

Gone, but her heart was still racing. They really were getting a little old for this sneaking around nonsense.

Sonora pulled a calm expression into place and opened the door to discover Yvette and Alex, the two of them wearing oversized grins.

"Yvette. Alex. Hi."

"Hi." Yvette looked a little contrite as she lifted a basket in the air slightly. "The shelter's locked, and I found some abandoned kittens."

"Oh. Of course. Come in." Sonora stepped aside and gestured them forward. She needed to time this properly so Ashton could leave before anyone noticed. "It'll just take me a minute to get my things."

"We can stay out here," Yvette offered.

"No, no. Definitely not. Come in out of the cold. I insist." Sonora all but attacked Alex. She caught his arm and jerked him into the house so she could shut the door firmly behind him. "Stay here."

She whirled on the spot, heading to the side wall where the winter boots and coats waited.

"How's your day going?" Alex asked.

Was that amusement in his tone? Did they know?

Well, if they did, chances were high they'd pretend not to, like everyone else in town. If *she* ignored the truck rolling nearly silently past her living room windows, so would they.

Still, Sonora adjusted position until Yvette and Alex had turned their backs toward the windows so they could keep facing her. People never failed to try and be polite. "Fine. Just being lazy."

She took as long as she could, leaving ample time for Ashton's truck to clear the drive. Then she headed out to the barn, welcoming the young couple into the sweet-smelling warmth.

"We're going to Rough Cut to load the charity food boxes," Yvette offered. "Thought we should drop these off before we went, though. I've given them their first shots, so that much is done."

"Any idea who left them with you? They were at the clinic, yes?" Sonora asked, slipping behind the desk and getting out the forms they needed.

"No idea who left them at my house," Yvette said. "Here, let us help."

They had all spent time dealing with the animal shelter since Sonora had set it up. A moment later Alex had grabbed one form, Yvette another, and the three of them all worked to quickly fill in the information that would be needed for eventual kitten adoptions.

The Ashton interruption pushed aside, Sonora focused on this good thing that was in her world. The animal shelter had given her motivation and a task to do well when she'd started to lose interest in other things.

She was needed here. She had a job to do, one that didn't involve sneaking around behind people's backs.

The thought shot into her like a lightning bolt. The glimpse of the truth that had eluded her for a long time.

Sonora hurried the young couple out the door a few minutes later, hoping to keep the thread of her thoughts alive long enough to finally nail down her concern. "I'll settle them. That's fine."

"Thanks for being here," Yvette said, stroking the kittens' soft ears one last time. "I'm glad we don't have to simply put sweet things like this down anymore."

"They'll make good mousers one day," Alex agreed.

Not even ten minutes later, Alex and Yvette were gone, and Sonora was alone in the quiet warmth of the shelter. The basket of purring kittens climbed over her fingers where she'd laid them in the furry mass, seeking comfort from the tactile life force.

Need.

The emotion had been a driving force in her for years. The shelter, spending time with her family, and helping her children and grandchildren to grow into healthy humans.

She'd been asked before why she'd lived with her daughter and helped raise the children. Because they'd needed her. It was part of what she'd always longed for. Worked for. Strived to provide.

Only, now she saw a different picture forming. Need was a nebulous beast. On one end of the spectrum, it meant being driven by duty. Trapped by onerous daily tasks that required time and took from a person no matter how the person giving felt.

At its best, though, need was the heart-and-soul connection Sonora had discussed with Ryan so long ago.

Dammit. How had she been so unobservant? Need was a part of love. Of loving someone. She stroked the ball of fur under her fingers and felt tears begin to rise.

She loved Ashton. She wanted him, not just physically but in her life. But he didn't need her. Not the same way. He'd shown that over and over during the past years, and she couldn't fight it anymore.

She loved him.

Which meant...

It took ages before the only thing that seemed to make sense solidified into stone. She loved him. If he loved her, that would be one thing. If he didn't, though, there was only one choice.

She'd have to let him go.

Hours later, Sonora still couldn't see another choice, no matter how much she tried to rearrange the puzzle pieces. She dreaded the next part of her life more than any moment since being forced to say a sudden goodbye to Greg.

It would be unkind to do this any way other than in person. Sonora pulled herself together and made her way to Silver Stone. Forgetting about parking on the sly, she pulled up right in front of Ashton's rooms, marched up to his door, and knocked.

He opened the door, his expression bright until he got a look at her face. "Sonora? Something wrong?"

"No. Yes. No," she insisted, folding her hands in front of her like a choirboy.

He gestured behind him. "Come in."

"No. I need to do this here." She took a deep breath. "I don't think I can see you anymore."

His jaw hung open. "Are you drunk?"

The urge to roll her eyes at him was so instinctive, she nearly cried. "I'm very sober and very serious." She met his gaze straight on. "I've been your friend for a very long time,

Ashton. And I've very much enjoyed being your lover. But we can't keep doing this."

"What are you talking about?" He stepped outside, no coat, no shoes. Stockinged feet in the snow of the porch as he shook his head in confusion. "You don't mean this. If you need time for yourself, that's fine, but—"

"I love you." She said it quietly, but the words echoed off the walls around them like a shout.

Ashton stilled. Went absolutely motionless.

Sonora held on to her courage and threw her pride to the wind. "If you love me too, then we have something to talk about."

He swallowed so hard. "*Sonora*."

She waited.

His face folded through a myriad of expressions, his thoughts as clear as if he'd spoken. Fear, confusion, anger—

Sadness.

"It's okay," she assured him quietly. "It's going to be okay."

She turned to go.

He caught her arm. "Don't leave. Come in. Let's talk about this."

Sonora patted the hand on her arm. "Let me go, Ashton."

She walked away.

And he let her.

THE GHOSTS OF CHRISTMAS FUTURE

Ashton wasn't sure what woke him, but the noise had been big enough to make him jump in his bed. Utter darkness pooled through the room, and dragging himself alert felt as if he were being pulled through molasses.

His head was fuzzy, and regret arrived hard and fast. Last night...

Right. Last night he'd been brooding. It had been three weeks since Sonora had shown up and tossed him into confusion and anger.

Three weeks where every time he thought about contacting her, his guilty-conscience stopped him before he hurt her further.

Last night he'd finally caved to frustration and tipped back a couple of extra-strong drinks.

"Not a young man anymore," he complained. He sat upright, and an icy chill wrapped boney fingers around him.

Cold.

No heat?

A quick glance to the side left him frowning. His digital clock was off.

Damn. A power outage meant he needed to haul ass and make sure things were okay in the barns. He fumbled in the dark to dress against the weather.

Outside the sky was an eerie shade of grey-black, with the blowing snow turning the world into an old black-and-white movie. Ashton marched across the yard, headed to the barn, when a grey-toned lantern bouncing that way caught his attention.

He met Caleb at the barn door. "Everything okay in the house?"

"For now. The girls are still asleep." There was ice in his tone, as if his rough edges had gone ragged. "You still plan to join us for Christmas dinner? Play the fiddle for the girls?"

"Always do," Ashton said easily. Caleb looked worn out and a hell of a lot older than the day before. "You not sleep well last night?"

"Never sleep well," Caleb grumbled. "Didn't help that Luke stopped by to tell me he's getting a divorce."

Ashton jerked to a stop. "The hell?"

Luke and Kelli *divorcing*? It was the last possible thing Ashton could imagine.

"Don't look so surprised," Caleb said. "It was doomed from the start, but he insisted Penny would change."

"Penny—" Ashton shook his head. Hell, he considered sticking a finger in his ears to clear out the cobwebs.

He eyed Caleb a little closer and wondered what exactly the other man had been up to that he thought Penny was still in the picture when Luke's ex-fiancée hadn't been around for years.

"Made pretty shitty tree-decorating conversation, I can tell you that. Then Walker called to say he's not coming this year. Dustin's already complaining about how much he'll have to do to help since the nanny went home to her parents for the holidays."

Ashton barely managed to keep from swearing. "*Nanny*?"

The Stone family hadn't had a nanny around since Tamara Coleman came and conquered, and she and Caleb had been married for over four years.

Caleb had his head turned to the breaker box and was grumbling madly as he flipped switches. "Should have known this one wasn't the type to stick around when we really needed her. Only nanny who had any kind of sense with the girls was Tamara—but look how that turned out."

Perfectly?

Ashton stared at Caleb harder. "Where is Tamara?"

A rude noise escaped the other man. "How the hell should I know? Probably married with a couple of kids by now. Not here, thank God."

This wasn't right. Nothing about this conversation was right.

Caleb flipped another couple of breakers. "Nope, things might be shitty this holiday, but damn if I was ever going to let myself get tied up again, let alone with some overbearing, opinionated, bossy woman who wanted to tell me how to run my ranch. Run my life." He pointed at Ashton. "You know what I'm talking about. You've said it many times. There's nothing a woman can bring except trouble. Don't need them. Don't want them."

THE LIGHTS WENT ON OVERHEAD, growing brighter and brighter until the room blurred...

"AND SOMETIME IN the new year, I want to talk about crew quarters." Tucker poured a little more coffee into Ashton's cup.

Ashton blinked, staring around in confusion. He was no longer in the barn with Caleb. The world was still an off-grey colour, but now his nephew sat in front of him in Ashton's own bunkhouse rooms.

The room seemed a little colder, though. No knickknacks, no crayon-scrawled art from the youngest of the Stone children on the fridge. Ashton twisted to examine his own home, shocked at the differences.

Bare and plain. The fluffy cushions were gone as well as the cozy blanket Sonora had insisted on bringing over so she wouldn't be cold when they watched shows together.

He rose to his feet and peered toward his bedroom, dismayed to discover his bed was covered with an old grey-and-blue quilt he'd owned for years instead of the new one Sonora had made him. Even the single macrame he'd kept—his favourite that looked like an owl—was missing from its place of honour.

"Uncle Ashton? You okay?" Tucker placed a hand on Ashton's shoulder and squeezed lightly. "Dipping into the Christmas cheer a little early?"

"No," Ashton insisted. He shook his head. "What were you saying?"

"Crew quarters. We've got more men coming on in the future, so I was thinking about a renovation project. Go for an actual bunkhouse for the newcomers and spruce up the old rowhouse for the longtime staff. And I'd like to adjust a set of rooms to match yours. I could use a little more space now that I'm here full time."

Tucker leaned back in his chair and sipped his coffee.

Ashton looked him over carefully, considering the suggestion. "Why do you need more room?"

Tucker snorted. "Because I'm not fifteen anymore? I'd like enough space to actually make it feel comfortable. Enough room to bring someone home every now and again."

Ashton thought his nephew must have a recent death wish. "You plan to bring anyone home, you best have your will up to date. Ginny will skin you alive, and *then* she'll get mean."

Tucker snorted. "What are you talking about? Haven't seen that woman in years. Not as if she has any say in how I run my life."

What. The. Hell? Ashton glared at his nephew. "Stop pulling my leg. It's not fucking funny anymore."

"And neither is you asking me bullshit questions about Ginny when you know it just makes me angry." Tucker's complaining grew louder, and fire flashed in his eyes. "She was a good time, all right? What we did was fun, but it was never meant to be anything more. You of all people should understand that."

Ice slid up Ashton's spine. "What does that mean?"

"You always said you would never tie yourself down. The fact you and Sonora fooled around for as long as you did surprised me a little, but I knew it wouldn't last. Someday she'd make demands, you'd refuse—that would be it. 'Last thing I want is to become my brother.'" Tucker shrugged. "That's what you always said. I never want to be my dad. In a relationship where I can't think without her permission. Can't breathe without someone getting mad at me. Can't just fucking live my life."

The longer Tucker spoke, the colder the room grew. The walls were washed with ice crystals, grey seeping into his nephew's face and hands.

"You and Ginny were always meant to be," Ashton insisted. "Any fool could see that."

"Ha, well, *this* fool saw a trap, just like you've always said. I got the hell out of there while I still had a chance." Tucker rose and slapped a hand on Ashton's shoulder. "If being alone is good enough for you, it's more than good enough for me."

The walls blurred, the world around him changing.

"No." Ashton shook his head, trying to clear the cobwebs. "No more of this hell."

But he was talking to the wind for all the good it did.

WHEN THE LIGHTS went back to normal, Ashton was driving up the road to Sonora's place. The barn had a new addition, and the house was freshly painted. Sonora's truck was nowhere to be seen. Instead, an SUV and an old Ford sat outside.

Ashton hurried through the grey to the front door, knocking impatiently.

The man who opened the door eyed him with suspicion. "Yeah?"

"Where's Sonora?"

The man frowned. "Who— Oh. Her." He cleared his throat uneasily. "You haven't been around for a while, have you?"

"Where is she?" Ashton demanded.

Yet without an answer, he knew. Whatever nightmare was happening, Ashton knew. He closed his eyes, and when he opened them again, he stood in the graveyard on the outskirts of Heart Falls.

A black marble stone lay at his feet.

He didn't want to look. Couldn't bear to witness what everything screamed he was about to see.

Sonora Fallen
Forever in Our Hearts

HE WOKE with his heart in his throat and a cry on his lips.

His watch said it was December twenty-third, and the schedule said he wasn't on shift until after lunch. His shaking hands said if he didn't find something to do, he would fall apart.

He quietly did a drive-by past Sonora's before anything else and took his first real breath of the morning when he spotted her truck parked in its usual spot.

When the afternoon rolled around, Ashton was still shaky and not sure what to do about the nightmare. What to do about her visit and the question she'd given him.

Why had she asked if he loved her? More importantly, why had he not answered?

Fighting the answers to both those questions was why he hid in a stall for a little horse therapy, aka, some monotonous, nerve-calming grooming.

Worked as good for him as for the horses.

He curried his favourite horse, the long peaceful sweeps of his arm like a smooth metronome pacing his breathing and his heart rate.

Could he survive without Sonora? No.

But did he love her?

A soft cough sounded from his right.

"Mind if I interrupt?" asked Yvette Wright, Alex's new sweetheart, although from the way the two of them had once constantly sparred with each other, Ashton had figured that partnership was a long shot.

Seemed Alex had better luck with Yvette than Ashton did with Sonora.

"You need my full attention, or can I finish working on Happy-Go-Lucky here?"

"Keep working. I need some information on Alex," she said quickly. "Personal stuff, which I know you can't usually hand out, but I'm really hoping you'll be okay bending the rules a little."

Ashton hesitated for a second before his fingers went back into motion. "Personal?"

Yvette glanced around to make sure they were alone. "I want to contact his parents for a surprise Christmas Day call, but I don't want to ask *him* for their number, because then it wouldn't be a surprise. What do you think?"

He considered. "Let me finish. I've got that information on file." Ashton's amusement rose. "I take it he's convinced you to keep going past December?"

"It was kind of hard to not be convinced. Not when the man pretty much started out telling me he thought we were supposed to be together."

Seemed too easy. "Was that all it took?"

Yvette considered hard then spoke slowly. "What I thought I needed a month ago is not what I truly needed. Alex has given me the time to figure that out, all the while making it very clear what *he* needs. We've still got stuff to work out in the future, but I think we plan to do it together."

The words landed on his ears then swooped through his brain like an owl on a field-mouse hunt. Ignoring the nearly violent urge to walk away so he could place all his attention on the revelation hovering just within reach, Ashton brushed his hands off and motioned toward the door. "Let me get that info for you."

The young woman was gone a few minutes later with her heart in her eyes and a smile on her lips.

Ashton didn't even try to go back to grooming. Instead he leaned on the wall in his office as his brain buzzed.

What I thought I needed...

What he said he needed...

Figure it out—together.

His head thumped against the wall.

What he'd said he needed—what they'd *both* said they needed at one point—had changed.

And way back at the beginning, she'd straight-up told him

what to do about those changes. Hadn't she? Was it really that simple? Could it be?

Only one way to find out.

Ashton grabbed his hat and coat and hurried out the door. He had plans to make happen and only a little time to arrange things.

Nightmares be damned. He'd seen what a future without Sonora looked like. No way on earth was he agreeing to that.

Not when what he needed to do was man up, start listening.

And offer one crystal clear confession.

14

---

*S*onora sat at the kitchen table with a teacup in hand and her gaze focused out the window. December thirty-first always made her contemplative. Usually she considered that a good thing.

This year she ached inside.

She hadn't seen Ashton more than in passing since their interrupted interlude at the start of the month. It had been easier than expected to avoid him. There had been a lot going on, and she'd deliberately chosen to spend more time with her daughter. She'd worked at Fallen Books. She'd volunteered at the Heart Falls Seniors Lodge. She'd even gone to visit with Rose and Tansy and helped during the holiday rush.

Malachi and Sophie had begun eyeing her suspiciously, but so far, her children had held their tongues.

No matter how hard she tried to hide it, something was clearly wrong. Not with Ashton or his response. Having him admit he was in love with her had been a one-in-a-million chance, and Sonora accepted that.

Yet things couldn't go on like this, Sonora decided. For both their sakes, she needed to find a way to stop brooding and make a new beginning. Ashton would be in her life. Small town, tangled families. He was a part of her world.

But they had to start again, and their new relationship would be built on respect and nothing more.

God, this was going to break her.

The sunshine in the window warmed her nearly as much as the heat from the wood-burning stove, and she closed her eyes and lifted her face to the light. Comfortable in body even as her mind raced through all the possibilities of how to approach the new year in a new way.

Which choices would leave her heart in fewer pieces?

"I know you can do it."

The unexpected voice made her jerk in her chair. She turned to discover a familiar man with blond hair smiling as he settled beside her. "Greg?"

Her husband took her hand as he leaned his elbows on the table. "Hello, sunshine."

"How—"

He poured himself a cup of tea then topped hers up. "You need someone to talk to. So let's talk."

Sonora glanced around the room. Still winter outside, still her cozy home inside. But Greg...

"So what if it's impossible? Sometimes impossible situations are the best kind there are," he teased before lowering his voice and speaking earnestly. "Your heart is aching. I hate seeing you like this."

The love in his eyes had always been there. Always been so bright and so constant. She'd never doubted him, not for a moment, through the ten years they'd shared.

"You know you're not really there," she insisted.

One shoulder lifted lazily. "I haven't been here for years, but you've still heard me. This isn't much different."

"You're sitting at my table," she pointed out. "But you're not real."

"Then you can't possibly upset me or hurt me. Roll with it already, Sonora. Let me help you figure this out."

Literally talking to her ghosts. Sonora sipped her tea and had to smile. "Okay. Let's figure this out."

"Why are you not with Ashton?"

Jeez. She dropped her cup to the table and glared at Greg. "Still with the in-my-face questions, ghost or visible."

"Best way to find the truth."

"Because he doesn't need me." She snapped the words then instantly regretted them. She squeezed her eyes shut and growled in frustration. "I want to be needed. I want to not just give but give in a way that builds happiness."

"And you don't think that's what you're doing?" Greg considered, his expression thoughtful. "No. The fooling around without labels or a true commitment had reached its expiration date."

"It really had," Sonora agreed softly.

"Smart woman." Greg stroked a strand of hair behind her ear. "Two things I admired most about you were how big your heart was and how smart you were in knowing how best to share your love."

"You never looked down on me. I realize now how rare that is, especially considering I was eighteen and you were thirty-four. You always said I could do anything, but you were there if heavy lifting was required."

"That wasn't all I wanted to do for you, but it was part of it." Greg rubbed his chin. "Why is this such a tangle for you? Why can't you simply love this Ashton of yours?"

"Because he doesn't love me," Sonora shared sadly.

"Are you sure?" Greg tapped his chest. "For some people, getting what's in here to pop out of our mouths is a tough task."

She supposed.

"You know what?" Greg leaned forward and spoke as if sharing a secret. "*I* think he loves you."

Not what she'd expected him to say. "You do?"

"Yup. He looks at you the same way I always did."

A gust of wind hit the house, and her bedroom door slammed shut. The bookcase beside it that held trinkets and family pictures rocked, and a couple of frames toppled to the floor.

Sonora hurried to pick them up and return them to where they belonged.

And froze.

The two frames in her hands were very different but equally special. One was an image from years ago of Greg with his arm around her. She had smiled at the camera, but his gaze was locked on her, his expression bright and pure, as if he would move mountains for her.

The other was an impulsive group shot during a Stone gathering where they'd all been in the barn after riding. Tamara had called them all together, and Sonora had ended up squeezed in between Tucker and Ashton.

Ashton was watching her, and his expression was so familiar it made her take a second look.

He looks at you the same way I always did.

Sonora glanced back at the table, but Greg wasn't there anymore. Only one teacup, the blanket that had been around her shoulders fallen to the chair seat when she'd stood…

Had she been asleep and dreamed the entire thing?

Maybe. But dreams sometimes came true.

Greg was right. She loved Ashton, period. Just like Greg had accepted her and simply loved her all those years ago, now it was her turn to push past her expectations.

She would take Ashton as he was, and together, they'd find a way.

Sonora hurried toward the kitchen to tidy up before driving to Silver Stone and tracking down the bastard. It was time to make up for the hurt she'd caused them both.

She had just lowered her cup into the sink when the front door opened, and a bright voice called out a greeting. "Hey, Grandma, where are you?"

Sonora stopped, surprise turning to happiness. "Rose. What are you doing here?"

Rose kicked off her boots then stepped into the room, holding out the bouquet in her hands. "I'm a delivery girl. This is for you."

"How sweet. Thank—"

"It's from Ashton."

Oh. Sonora's hands fell to her sides.

Rose grinned. "You should see your face right now."

"I can only imagine," Sonora mumbled.

Her granddaughter pulled a blue envelope from her pocket. "And this is for you as well."

Sonora should have sat. Should have taken the flowers from Rose and given her a hug hello.

Instead, she all but shredded the envelope to get at the letter inside.

Sonora.

I'd like to take the easy way out and tell you everything in this note, but since nothing between us has ever been easy, I figure this shouldn't be either.

I've been rash. So have you, but in the end, I refuse to allow the best thing I've ever been given to slip from my life. I've seen a future without you, and it's the closest thing to hell that I can imagine.

Won't you please join me for a fresh start? Tomorrow, a new year begins, and it seems an appropriate time for us to find a way to make the path forward smoother.

Wear something pretty—but then, you always look beautiful. I'll wash up the best I can, but you know this ugly mug only improves so much with soap and water.

And now I'm rambling because that's what you do to me.

I love you.

I know, foolish that the first time I tell you is in a letter, but I figured if I didn't put it down in writing, you'd never agree to meet my sorry ass.

I plan to tell you again in person, and more, tomorrow when we meet. The church doors will be unlocked, and I'll be in the sanctuary, praying for wisdom and patience.

Noon. I hope you'll come.

I'd demand you show up, but even I finally know better than that.

Yours,
Ashton

Sonora lifted her gaze from the note. How could mere letters formed into words on the page make her heart race?

Her granddaughter stood there, the bouquet in her hands and a gentle smile on her face. "Did you read this?" Sonora asked.

"Of course not." Rose's lips twitched as she tried to keep a straight face. "Well, except for the part where he asked how to spell *appropriate* and then made me proofread the entire note for spelling mistakes." Her smile widened. "He loves you, Grandma."

The words would never get old, but Sonora wanted to hear

them from his lips, not someone else's. Not just on a page. "I know he does. I love him too."

The young woman eyed her for a moment then moved decisively. Rose marched to the sink and pulled out the kitchen shears before taking a glass vase from the top of the cupboard. While she trimmed and arranged the flowers, she spoke softly. "I've always admired how there's no stopping you. You decide on a thing, and it gets accomplished. No matter the obstacles."

A snort escaped. This one was as silver-tongued as her father. "Are you calling your granny stubborn?"

Rose wiped her cheek with the back of her hand. "That's a laugh. I might be brave enough to call you *stubborn*, but I'd *never* attempt to call you *Granny*."

Good point. Sonora slipped beside her granddaughter and leaned on the counter. "Do you think his note is romantic?"

"What matters is what *you* think," Rose returned. "But, Grandma, you've been tangling with Mr. Stewart for as long as I can remember. And I'm old enough to know that *tangling* these days involves more than pretending to bicker at barbecues and offering silly presents to annoy each other."

"Sex doesn't leave the picture when you turn thirty," Sonora said dryly.

"Thank goodness, or I'd be in trouble." Rose winked. "Your single granddaughters don't see a lot of action these days. Which is sad, especially comparing Tansy and my love lives to yours."

She looked away, but amusement curled her lips.

"You're nothing but mischief," Sonora complained even as she pulled Rose into an embrace. "First, you're a beautiful woman. Someone is going to truly see you one day soon and fall head over heels in love. You'll probably make your father pull out his hair by falling so fast that you're still spinning when you and your young man say *I love you*."

"Are you an oracle now?" Rose asked, but she squeezed

Sonora tightly. "I hope you're right. But in the meantime, Tansy and I have plans for expanding the shop. Ivy and Walker have plans to expand their family, and that will be exciting and new. And you—"

Rose pulled away and met Sonora's gaze straight on. She lifted the note from Ashton in the air and waved it gently.

"And I have a decision to make," Sonora said.

"Do you though? Do you really?" Rose asked quietly. "Or do you simply need to admit you've already decided so we can go pick out what you'll wear tomorrow?"

Her granddaughter was wise beyond her years.

15

January 1, United Church sanctuary. Noon.

*W*aiting had been hell, but as the door opened, Ashton realized there was one thing worse. Not knowing exactly what would happen during the next moments was even more nerve-racking.

Heart pounding, he stepped toward where light spilled through the opening church door.

Sonora stepped into the sunshine and dazzled him where he stood.

He'd wondered if she might leave her hair down. Maybe pull on a clean pair of jeans and frilly blouse. But instead of pants, she wore a dress of the palest cream. Ivory, maybe—he wasn't good with colours—but it contrasted sweetly with the silvery sheen of the braids coiled on her head like a crown. She looked amazing.

Sonora moved cautiously toward him as if worried he might

bolt. Her gaze drifted down then up, and he nervously straightened his tie and stood a little taller.

The silence changed. No longer was it about waiting, hope and fear swirling together. Instead, the air crackled with anticipation and excitement. Seconds pounded past. Her footsteps on the carpet echoed like boots on concrete.

Sonora stopped a foot away from him, the corner of her lips curling as she lifted her chin and met his gaze.

So strong. So wonderful, and *here*—standing before him. Just what he'd hoped and yet not dared to believe could happen.

Ashton took a deep breath. Let it out slowly.

"I love you."

They said it at the same moment then laughed, the overlapping responses like mirror-perfect images.

Sonora caught his hand in hers and brought it to her lips. "I knew what you meant. When you said to meet you here at the church, I knew it wasn't just…"

Her voice broke, and damn if he didn't have to blink hard himself.

"Stubborn old brain of mine." Ashton pressed his thumb to her cheek and wiped away the tear rolling down the surface. "You told me. You told me years ago that marriage was for two people who were in love. That love was what made people book a church and say *I do*."

"Is that what we're going to do?" Sonora squared her shoulders. "I love you, Ashton. But I've thought about it over the past days. It wasn't fair of me to cut you off without talking things through. And I've decided that I don't need anything official. If you love me, if you want to be with me, that's enough."

"I do love you. Can't believe it took me this long to spit the damn words out."

Her shoulders shook.

"To say it, I mean." He sighed heavily, exasperated with himself. "*Saying* is more romantic than talk of spitting and such."

This time she laughed out loud before smiling softly. "I don't blame you for hesitating to say it. You were worried about —*things*."

Her giving heart was trying to make this easier on him. As if allowing him to skip the confession.

He did it anyway. "There's no excuse. For me to look at my brother then cry off on marriage because of him? That's not as smart as I'd like to claim to be. His marriage is only one example. So many others I've witnessed over the years have been good."

"But when family fails, it cuts deep. Plus, your best friend, and Caleb's first marriage." Sonora nodded, expression going thoughtful. "But yes. You've also had good examples. The Stones, the Fords."

"Caleb and Tamara. Ivy and Walker. Your daughter, Sophie, and Malachi." Ashton caught both Sonora's hands in his. "Luke and Kelli. Tucker and Ginny—although they're not married yet, but they're headed there."

"It's wonderful when the children lead the way."

He hummed. "They got there because they already had a road to follow. Every time you've spoken about Greg, it's been clear that his love has held you solid. He's been gone for more years than you had together, and he's still sharing his love." Thoughtfulness drifted in his eyes before he met hers again. "I don't know how long we'll have together, but I hope I can uphold that legacy and make it stronger."

"We'll build on it together," she insisted.

An echo of the words he'd heard from Yvette a week ago. "Together."

Then he got down on one knee, keeping her hand in his. "Sonora Fallen, I love you. You once agreed to be my friend and then my lover. Now I need you to say yes to letting everyone know you're my heart. Marry me?"

Sonora pressed her free hand briefly to her mouth then nodded enthusiastically. "Yes."

He tugged her to his level and caught her lips in a kiss, because no matter what else had to still happen, this was the most important.

God, he'd missed her. The days of being apart had made it clear that while he still might have to slap down uncomfortable habits, his concerns weren't with Sonora.

With her mouth on his, the entire world shifted back into proper alignment.

He softened the kiss until they paused, foreheads touching. Staring into each other's eyes.

"I have some things planned," he said quietly. "It's kind of bossy of me, but I thought if our meeting went well, I should run with it before you come to your senses."

She laughed. "Bossy? Like what?"

He pulled out his phone and shook it. "I told the pastor that if you agreed to marry me, I'd text him. He'll come and do our vows right now."

"Text him? I'm very impressed."

"For you, anything."

"Tell me what other mischief you've organized." Her expression was sheer delight.

"The wedding, and I might have booked us a honeymoon."

Her jaw dropped. "You're kidding."

"Not kidding. So I'm really hopeful you don't have anything else planned, because we're past the cancellation date for any kind of a refund."

Laughter burst free. Sonora threw her arms around his neck and squeezed so tight for a moment that he could barely breathe.

He was just fine with that.

"Does this mean yes to the wedding? Yes to the honeymoon?"

She stood and pulled him to his feet as well. "One second."

She pulled her phone from some hidden place and tapped a few keys before pushing it back into her hidden pocket.

Then she caught his hands in hers. "Now then, I'm very happy you were bossy, but I need to admit that I was as well."

Ashton wasn't sure where she was going with this. "How?"

"First things first. Yes to the honeymoon."

His turn to chuckle. "That's top priority? Good by me, but just checking for clarity."

"The other matter is, yes, we can get married now, but I'd like to have my son-in-law do the vows. Plus, do you mind if I invited a few people?"

He paused, thinking of Tucker, his friends, the people he'd like to have as witnesses—

The sanctuary doors opened, and a crowd poured in.

The first man in the lineup was Tucker, Ginny on his arm, and they stepped into the aisle and approached like a train on fire.

Tucker's smile flashed bright as he shook Ashton's hand. "Congrats, Uncle. You finally got the girl."

Ashton didn't claim to be the sharpest tool in the shed, but it didn't take too much mental power to put two and two together. "You knew." He glanced between Tucker and Ginny, who was hugging Sonora, and then poked Tucker in the chest. "When you texted to ask if I wanted you here, Sonora had already put out a call for people to be ready."

"Well, partly right. I did know, but it was Fern who called me and the others." Tucker's grin only got wider. "Seems Rose knew something was up, and she told Tansy, who told Fern. The baby of the family was the one to ask Sonora if it was okay to invite the potential wedding guests."

Fern. Of course, Fern. Ashton didn't know her as well as he

wanted to yet, but Sonora said she was whip smart and determined to boot.

They'd make time to have the girls over—

It hit. Goddamn, one more unexpected truth finally sank into his thick skull, and he froze.

Tucker frowned. "Uncle Ashton?"

Ashton clutched Tucker's hand. "I'm going to be a grandpa."

A soft note of approval flowed from his nephew, and then a solid hand landed on his shoulder and squeezed tight. "I guess you are. Those girls are damn lucky. You've already proved you know how to be a father figure a hundred times over. Grandpa is supposed to be even better. More spoiling, less responsibility."

Ashton wasn't sure about that last part, but Sonora had drifted back to his side and slipped her fingers around his arm, and suddenly the crowded room was the least of his concern.

She was going to be his. That was all he wanted.

First though, they actually needed to get hitched.

Only it wasn't going to be simple as the church continued to fill with friends and family and people from the community. Everyone swarmed around them, because it seemed the rule of the day was to offer congratulations before they'd even said *I do*. Ashton shook hands and accepted back pats and teasing comments about getting his act together.

Gary Silver hugged him so tight Ashton's ribs creaked. "Good to know you figured it out in the end."

"Old dog, new tricks," Ashton deadpanned. Sonora elbowed him gently in the ribs, and he grunted before grinning. "Not-so-old dog, new tricks."

"Better," she said, pausing to hug Gary tightly. "Thanks for being there for him all these years."

"I'll say the same for you." Gary winked then went to join Brooke and Mack, who had already offered their greetings.

The rest of Ashton's friends from the fire hall arrived. Alex and Yvette strode up hand in hand, and the starstruck expression on the man's face gave Ashton a blast of sheer amusement. At least until Ashton realized his face was probably a mirror image.

Ryan carefully escorted a very pregnant Madison, her belly pushing forward with what seemed like impossible proportions.

Ashton hurried to help her into the nearest pew so she wouldn't get jostled. "Nice to see you here, but are you sure it's a good idea to be out these days?"

"I still have two weeks to go," Madison said, hand resting on her belly. "Now is the occasion for distractions. So thanks for arranging the wedding—perfect timing, really. And tomorrow we're having a girls' night out activity. Making belly casts."

"Never certain what those should be used for. Chips would be good. Or a punch bowl." Alex eyed Madison's belly. "Swimming pool?"

Yvette tugged Alex's arm, rolling her eyes at him. "Your mouth is going to get you hurt someday." She smiled at Ashton and Sonora. "We're so happy for you."

"Thanks, darling," Sonora replied.

"By the way, you were right." Ashton caught Yvette's hand firmly and gave it a good squeeze. "Brilliant in fact."

Yvette blinked. "I was?"

"Yup. So thanks for the advice."

Alex's curiosity was written in plain sight. "What did she tell you?"

"Well, that would be gossiping, and I don't agree with that." Ashton drawled the words then twisted with Sonora on his arm. "Come on. I want to make this official before you come to your senses."

Sonora snickered softly but willingly walked by his side as he guided her to the front of the chapel, where her granddaughters had been setting things in place. "What *did* Yvette tell you?"

"That knowing what we need is important but making decisions together is even better." He leaned in and whispered in her ear, "Making it cryptic is just to yank Alex's chain. He needs to be kept on his toes."

Which meant that Sonora was laughing as Ashton pulled her to a stop in the center of a circle of brilliant blooms. Hand in hand they waited as the room around them slowly quieted and everyone found a place to sit.

Finally, Sophie and Malachi stepped forward.

Sonora's daughter held out another bouquet as she snuck in for a hug from her mom. "I'm so happy for you." Sophie tossed a smile Ashton's direction. "For you both."

Before Ashton could say anything, Sophie slipped away to join the rest of the family in a nearby pew, and Malachi took her place, his grin entirely too big for such a solemn setting. He kissed Sonora's cheek then shook Ashton's hand.

He turned to face the gathering, smile flashing bright. "We are gathered here today to witness the wedding vows of Sonora Fallen and Ashton Stewart." He met Ashton's gaze. "*Finally.*"

Laughter rose and Ashton joined in. The amusement wasn't against them; it was *with* them.

He held Sonora's fingers in his, and she smiled as she gazed into his eyes, the love shining there as bright as the sunlight sparkling through the stained-glass windows. The vows they spoke were simple but heartfelt.

It was love. That was all they needed.

EPILOGUE

The breeze blowing in the window of their Hawaiian condo barely registered on her heated skin. Sonora wore a layer of sweat from Ashton's vigorous attentions. His hands, his tongue. His cock.

Her breath caught in her throat as Ashton pushed in again. Muscles gone slack from pleasure, Sonora gripped his wrists and held on as the pulses grew more demanding.

A rumbling groan trembled on the air as he slowed, and she dragged her eyes open to prepare for whatever trouble he was about to cause. Years of being lovers and yet she'd had no idea what this man was capable of when given days of uninterrupted time.

The honeymoon was a hit as far as she was concerned.

"I'm not going anywhere." Ashton spoke softly as he adjusted their position and broke the connection where she clutched him. He threaded their fingers together then pressed her hands to the mattress beside her head, staring into her eyes as they shared pleasure.

As they made love.

Oh, it was still sex, sometimes wild and untamed and raw.

But now it was clear the sweet and soft and tender fit with the rest of it hand in glove because of the truth at the heart of them.

Love.

Sonora accepted his kiss, raising her hips to meet his increasingly needy thrusts. Sinking into rapture as his body and hers tilted past the point of no return.

Breathless, they lay on the mattress and let the trade winds caress them. Sonora cuddled in tighter and sighed with contentment. "You are amazing."

"That's my line." Ashton kissed her forehead.

"No, seriously, I enjoyed what we had before, but this?" She cupped his cheek and offered a saucy grin. "You've upped your game. I like it."

"Maybe it's the extra sleep I'm getting."

"Then I'm making Tucker adjust your work schedule from now to eternity."

Ashton was still chuckling when he pulled her off the mattress and into the shower to clean up.

Hand in hand, they walked the beach outside the apartment, a slow stroll so unlike both of their get-it-done strides that Sonora had to laugh. "You think anyone would believe this?"

Ashton glanced at her, one brow raised. "That I'm dazzling everyone on the island with my neon-white legs?"

"Hey, you're starting to get some colour." Although she had to admit he had amusing tan lines. "Your legs will never be as dark as your arms or the back of your neck, though. Not unless you do chores all summer while wearing shorts."

"That'll never happen. I dislike getting scratched other than by your nails on my back. Or my ass."

A sharp inhale and then laughter drifted from a pair of younger couples passing in the opposite direction. Sonora was as close to giggling as she'd ever been in her life. "You're terrible."

"They looked as if they needed to know that old people—sorry, *older* people—still have sex." Ashton squeezed her fingers, pacing closer to the water's edge and allowing the tide to tickle them on every sweep. "Back to your comment, what won't people believe?"

"That we're relaxing. That you haven't spent hours devising a system to de-sand us every time we return from the beach. You slept in until eight this morning, and we had second coffees on the lanai. No agenda, no to-do list. I'm proud of you."

Ashton pulled her to a stop and twisted until they stood side by side facing the west. The ocean surface shimmered with dancing lights, the sun slowly descending toward the horizon and the thin strands of clouds waiting there. With his arm around her, Sonora rested her head on his shoulder.

Content. Right where she needed to be.

He pressed his lips to the top of her head and hummed softly. "I *have* a to-do list, though. One that's smarter and better than any I've ever jotted down."

"Oh?"

To their right, a family had gathered to enjoy the sunset as well, and childish laughter and screams rose skyward as two toddlers splashed in the surf and raced from incoming waves.

The dad swooped in a second before the littlest one got knocked on their butt, swinging the child in a circle then flying them into their mom's arms. The other child raced to join the group hug, and the lot of them collapsed to the sand in a pile of giggles.

Ashton turned her to face him. "Like that. Just being together in a way that makes them happy. We've enjoyed time together over the years, but it's been more by chance than deliberately. Not anymore. I want to be there for you, and I *need* you to be there for me. You're first on my to-do list from now on, Sonora. Always, I promise."

Could she feel any more happiness without bursting? "I love you."

"Good." He grinned when she wrapped her arms around his waist and stuck out her tongue. "I love you too, Mrs. Stewart."

The sunset was probably very beautiful that night, but Sonora missed the actual moment the sun dipped beneath the waves. She was too busy being kissed senseless.

She liked his new to-do list.

~

COMING BACK to snowy Alberta after his birthday mid-January was just mean. Although Ashton had missed the ranch, it was good to know that he wasn't needed every moment of every day anymore.

He couldn't even find it in him to be annoyed when everywhere he went around Silver Stone, the hands grinned widely and snickered before pulling themselves together.

"You both done working already?" Ashton asked Tucker when he ran into his nephew and Luke chatting easily together inside the main barn.

"Never done, you know that," Tucker said seriously. "Just making sure we also focus on the important stuff, like you taught us."

Luke winked at Ashton then ducked around Tucker. "Excuse me. Important stuff headed my way."

When he caught his wife, Kelli, up in a hug and spun her hard, Tucker just grinned harder.

Ashton shook his head. Kids. Didn't matter that they were in their thirties—they weren't getting any easier to understand.

He eyed Tucker. "Did I miss something?"

"Not yet," Tucker assured him. "Just a little competitive nature raising its head. You know how it is."

Right now? Ashton didn't have a clue. But then again, maybe he liked it that way...

The other thing he definitely liked was the change in his routine. While he and Sonora had been honeymooning, Tucker and Caleb had rewritten the schedule. Then they'd told Sonora his new hours.

She gloated the entire first full day they were home. "I'll be out the door before you some days," she teased.

"Not likely." He pulled her into his lap at the breakfast table and stole another kiss. "I feel bad. Like I'm taking advantage of them and only working half the time."

Sonora stroked Ashton's cheek. "I'm pretty sure they're just making up for all the days you worked *more* than a regular shift."

True. Plus, extra time in bed in the morning with Sonora was not a thing to hurry away from.

With his new routine, they shared breakfast and dinner every day. He still went to the ranch, and she worked the animal shelter and spent time in town with the family. A sweet pattern began to fall into place, and Ashton appreciated so much about their new stage of life.

There were still questions they had to deal with. Sonora's reference regarding how long she wanted to remain in charge of the animal shelter was one of them.

"Over the years I've had a couple of people ask about buying the farm and shelter, but I wasn't ready to give it up," she mentioned one night while they were preparing to go out.

"Are you now?" he asked.

Sonora considered then shook her head. "No. I'm still needed, and I'm still enjoying it, but it's not a forever thing,"

"You're good at it too," Ashton told her with complete honesty. "Maybe at some point we can arrange to give the work to others."

"Maybe." Sonora tugged him close for a kiss. "That's a

problem for another day, though. Come. Let's get ready for the party."

In their bedroom, Ashton finished dressing before her. Settled on the bed, he leaned back and enjoyed the view as she came out of the bathroom after her shower.

"Don't rush on my account," he told her cheekily.

Sonora winked then stripped off her robe and went to the closet for her outfit. He helped her change the light bandage over her new tattoo, happy to see it was healing well.

He'd been surprised to discover she'd made the booking while they were in Hawaii, and a couple of weeks after their return, she'd gotten new work done.

His name now formed a wave that crested just above her bikini line, and once she was given the go-ahead, he couldn't wait to kiss the hell out of the spot en route to other sweet pleasures.

But tonight was a celebration of another sort. The fire hall team Ashton worked with had organized a supervisory-staff party. The gathering was adults only, except for baby Justin, who had made his arrival the day Ashton and Sonora had been flying to the islands.

Brad and Hanna pulled up to Brooke and Mack's home in Heart Falls at the same time Sonora and Ashton did. Handshakes ensued even though he and Brad had seen each other only hours earlier.

"I brought the chocolate cake you like, Ashton," Hanna informed him.

"You sweet-talking my husband?" Sonora asked with a laugh as she handed him a blanket wrapped Crock-Pot.

"Sweet-feeding, more like." Hanna patted Ashton on the shoulder. "Crissy says you're her favourite."

"That's because he took her class on a tour of the fire hall and let them try the fire pole," Brad said before adding a complaint. "I wasn't allowed to use the pole when I was in grade six."

"I bet you weren't nearly so demanding," Ashton offered. "They were into everything, and I could barely keep up. Horses are far easier to wrangle."

Inside, the house was warm and smelled wonderful with a scent of spice on the air. Everyone gathered in the kitchen, some working, some relaxing.

Madison held little Justin in her arms with Ryan hovering at her side. They stood beside the island and visited with Alex and Mack as the men stirred pots on the stove. Beyond them, Brooke and Yvette set the table, cutlery clinking softly. Brooke's maternity top swayed as she moved, the curve of her belly beginning to show.

Sonora went straight to Madison and commandeered the baby. "He's darling."

"Good timing on your getaway. You managed to miss all the excitement," Ryan teased Ashton.

"I'll catch the next one," Ashton promised before giving Madison a side hug. "You did good, Mama. Pretty baby. I can already see he's going to bring joy to everyone around him. Just like you."

Madison's face contorted a split second before she burst into tears. An instant later she buried her face against Ryan's chest.

Ryan patted her back soothingly even while he nodded at Ashton. "Damn, you're good."

"Silly hormones," Madison complained when she finally pulled back and wiped at her eyes.

"Don't you try to explain away happy tears." Sonora bumped her hip against Madison's. "He's right. You and Ryan made a pretty baby, but the building never stops. It's guiding them as they grow up and become wonderful people that's the real trick."

"Good thing there are more kids on the way," Alex announced, a gleam in his eyes. "Just to make sure they have friends to share that growing up with."

Everyone froze, considering what he meant.

Madison blinked hard then held up a hand. "Not me. Good grief, that would be like the world's fastest conception. Also, immaculate conception at this point."

Ryan laughed. "There is that fact..."

"Then who? Other than Brooke, obviously." Sonora eyed the other two women. "Not me. I do not plan to hit the Guinness record book for being the oldest mother recorded, plus I decided a long time ago my womb was a no-parking zone."

"Mine still has a No Space Available sign as well," Yvette offered. "Give us time to enjoy just being a couple for a bit first, please."

All eyes flipped to Hanna and Brad.

Brad lifted her hand and kissed her fingers gently. "Alex spilled the beans, not me."

She rolled her eyes. "You men gossip far too much during night shifts at the fire hall."

"Oh, come on. They gossip just as much during the day shifts," Brooke pointed out before diving forward to offer a hug. "Hurrah for another baby on the way."

Conversation, celebration. An evening full of everything Ashton could have wanted, especially with Sonora by his side.

At one point, Alex elbowed him softly then tilted his head to where the ladies were all enthusiastically discussing some topic. "Marriage looks good on you. And her. I'm glad for you both."

"You got someone special as well." Ashton lifted his chin toward Yvette. "Never dreamed you'd pull it off."

"We're both lucky bastards, aren't we?" Alex sighed happily.

"That we are."

Good people, good friends.

They spent time with others and time alone. Ashton did his best to make Sonora's birthday on February first a memorable one. She took him to visit the newest members of the Stone/Fields family. The little girls Walker and Ivy had adopted were adorable tykes, and Ashton was tickled to discover he wasn't only a grandpa now, but a great-grandpa.

He gloried in crawling on the floor and pretending to be a horse for them. He also might have had an uncharitable thought or two aimed at his brother steal through his brain.

Take that, Steve, and shove it, Mr. You-Don't-Have-Kids-and-I-Do.

It was after another gathering of good people that the final seeds for change were planted. They'd just celebrated Tucker and Ginny's long-awaited wedding, and in the quiet after the family dinner, only four of them remained.

Ashton and Sonora. Caleb and Tamara. Two generations of Silver Stone overseers. Ashton, the last remaining member of the original crew. Caleb, solidly representing the next foundation stone.

Tucker and Ginny's wedding had formally united their families, and the moment felt huge. Even more so because the two of them had set their wedding day on the anniversary of the accident.

Fifteen years had passed since losing so much. Fifteen years of learning and growing and pulling together to get to this point.

Tamara leaned against Caleb's side then focused on Ashton. "Ginny shared something a few weeks ago that she found in her mom's journals. A plan Deb and Walter had discussed for

Silver Stone's future. Some of which you know because you were in on the early conversations."

Some of the future the Stones had dreamed of hadn't been possible. Yet, looking back, Ashton could honestly say he'd done what he could to make other parts of it happen. "They were the best of people, your folks."

"They were." Caleb dipped his chin firmly. "But now we're talking about you. And the fact they had discussed ideas for when you wanted to do the next thing."

Ashton blinked. "Me?"

Tamara nodded. "Retirement packages, some of which Silver Stone built into the payment schedule, but there's one new bit of information Ginny discovered that we really liked." She glanced at Caleb.

He cleared his throat. "I'm sorry we never discussed this before, because we should have. It's a good idea that's waited too long to happen. There's a section of land Dad thought you'd like to build a house on. It's got a view of the lake and a chunk of the river to the north. So if Sonora can convince you to not work all the time, you can always go fishing."

Ashton froze. "Land? Here on Silver Stone?"

"This place has been your home longer than it's been any of ours," Caleb pointed out.

"If you decide you'd prefer to stay at Sonora's place, we'll help with that instead," Tamara offered, slipping her hand briefly over Sonora's. "But you both clearly love living in the country. We'll make that work for you as long as possible."

Their own place on Silver Stone land. Ashton's throat went dry as a bone. He pulled Sonora closer. Not speaking—not trying to speak, because frankly nothing would have made it past his lips right then.

Sonora squeezed him tightly then sweetly turned to Caleb and Tamara. "Thank you. From both of us. It's not only a house you're offering but a home. We know that."

Ashton nodded, still not trusting his voice.

But then again—he *did* trust his voice. With everything in him.

Sonora could speak up and say what they needed because for so many years, she'd listened and learned, and every single thing she did was meant to make him happy.

Ashton stood then caught Caleb's hand and used it to pull the young man into a tight embrace. Sonora hugged Tamara, and around them, the world seemed a little brighter than before.

That night back at the house, Ashton took Sonora in his arms. "About the offer from the kids."

He stopped and shook his head.

"Go on. They'll always be *the kids* to us both." She shrugged. "I'm not saying we're old, but we certainly are older."

"That we are." Ashton took a slow look around the room. At the comfortable place where Sonora had lived for so many years. They both had memories from there. Good ones, and tough ones. First times, and fights, and lots and lots of laughter.

He had memories from the bunkhouse, but those were— different. He had no connections he'd miss by moving elsewhere.

Which was what he had to make clear to her now.

Ashton swung a finger around them, pointing to the walls, the windows, all of it. "We don't need to build somewhere new, you know. You have this place, and it's comfortable and cozy. More, though, it's been an important part of your life. I don't want you to give it up if you don't want to."

Sonora cupped his cheek. "I know. But this place is also more than what it started out as. Back when I bought it, it was about finding my independence and making a fresh start. Now it's also an animal shelter and a community gathering place, and sometimes it's bigger than what I need. But maybe it's just the right size for someone else." She glanced around at the snug setting then back into his eyes. "It was a good home. It *is* a good home, but it's only four walls. You're my heart, and together, *we* are what will make any place into a home."

He kissed her knuckles.

"Also, we could plan the new house to require fewer chores *and* include a bigger bathtub. Yes?"

He outright chuckled. "Yes."

Silence fell. The fire crackled as Sonora curled up on the couch beside him and they both read quietly. The peacefulness was night and day from the quiet evenings he'd spent alone in his bunkhouse rooms for so many years.

Fuller. Brighter. More.

She loves you, and I'm glad. It's your job to love and care for her from now on, all right?

Ashton glanced around, wondering who'd spoken. No one else was in the room. No music played, no phones nearby. Only him, Sonora, and Beauty curled up by the fire, sighing contentedly as only an old dog could.

Was he hearing things? Maybe.

But the words echoed in his head, and he accepted them as truth right to the core of his soul. Loving Sonora was what he'd always been meant to do.

He caught her fingers in his and held on tight.

She twisted toward him, one brow raised in question.

He lifted her chin and stroked her cheek in a gentle caress. "Just talking to a ghost. Explaining how much I love you."

Her eyes widened for a moment, and then his lips were on hers. A kiss. And another. He didn't plan to stop. Not the kissing or the loving.

From now to forever.

New York Times Bestselling Author Vivian Arend
invites you to Heart Falls. These contemporary ranchers live in
a tiny town in central Alberta, tucked into the rolling foothills.
Enjoy the ride as they each find their happily-ever-afters.

Holidays at Heart Falls
A Firefighter's Christmas Gift
A Soldier's Christmas Wish
A Hero's Christmas Hope
A Cowboy's Christmas List
A Rancher's Christmas Kiss

The Stones of Heart Falls
A Rancher's Heart
A Rancher's Song
A Rancher's Bride
A Rancher's Love
A Rancher's Vow

The Colemans of Heart Falls
The Cowgirl's Forever Love
The Cowgirl's Secret Love
The Cowgirl's Chosen Love

ABOUT THE AUTHOR

New York Times and *USA Today* bestselling author Vivian Arend loves to share the products of her over-active imagination with her readers. She writes contemporary, western, and light-hearted paranormal romances. The stories are humorous yet emotional, usually with a large cast of family or friends, and a guaranteed happily-ever-after. Vivian lives in British Columbia, Canada, with her husband of many years—her inspiration for every hero and a willing companion for all sorts of adventures.

www.vivianarend.com